D0615714

Place Names

Place Names

A BRIEF GUIDE TO TRAVELS IN THE BOOK

Jean Ricardou

TRANSLATED BY JORDAN STUMP

Dalkey Archive Press

CHAMPAIGN AND LONDON

Originally published in French as *Les lieux-dits*
by Éditions Gallimard (1969)
Copyright © 1969 by Éditions Gallimard
Translation copyright © 2007 by Jordan Stump

First English translation, 2007
All rights reserved

Library of Congress Cataloging-in-Publication Data
Ricardou, Jean.
[Lieux-dits. English]
Place names : a brief guide to travels in the book /
Jean Ricardou ; translated by Jordan Stump.
p. cm.
ISBN-13: 978-1-56478-478-0 (alk. paper)
ISBN-10: 1-56478-478-9 (alk. paper)
I. Stump, Jordan, 1959– II. Title.
PQ2678.I22651.L513 2007
843'.914—dc22 2007025353

This work has been published, in part, thanks to the
French Ministry of Culture—National Book Center.

Partially funded by a grant from the Illinois Arts Council, a state
agency, and by the University of Illinois, Urbana-Champaign

DALKEY ARCHIVE PRESS
University of Illinois
605 E. Springfield, MC-475
Champaign, IL 61820

www.dalkeyarchive.com

Design and composition by Quemadura
Printed on permanent/durable acid-free, recycled paper,
bound in the United States of America, and
distributed throughout North America and Europe

FOR ED. WORD.

Contents

With them, everything is ordered, impersonal; not one tensed muscle, not one rolled eye that does not seem to belong to a sort of deliberate mathematics, which guides everything, and through which everything passes.

ARTAUD

Place Names

Bannière

No sooner has this dark ridge been traversed, beneath the clouded skies, than a glistening appears on the landscape below. Its rolling terrain flattened by this view from above, the valley of Bannière offers a host of discreet undulations to the traveler's gaze. On either side of the river lies a series of woods and open fields, alternating with near perfect regularity, forming a grid. Through this design the region's farmers aim to conserve, despite multiple calcareous outcrops, a moisture beneficent for their pastures.

A curious fact: the silken water that flows through these antithetical verdures is known as the Damier, or "Checkerboard." Like many another in the province, this name has long excited the passions of scholars. As might well be surmised, these fall into two camps, irreconcilably opposed. The one vaunts the virtues of realism: however complex a word's family tree, its branching genealogy can always be followed back to the origin. In this case, the problem is elementary indeed: no doubt the river took its name from the strange countryside that it irrigates; it was "the river of the *damier*," and hence, very simply, the Damier. Certain subtle embellishments, dangerous because valid only in this sin-

Bannière

gle instance, have at times been appended to that basic motivation: for instance, that the name's transference from banks to river replicates the reflective phenomenon by which a watercourse, burrowing virtual depths into its own level surface, borrows the colors and forms of the landscape around it.

The other clan grounds itself in the inalienable rights of poetry. Illusory, they claim, is any search for the origins of words, for words are the provenance of things. Their solution is easily deduced.

Implanted on a bend in the river, Bannière unites some eighty slate-roofed abodes on the Damier's convex bank. Ribbons of smoke rise in all seasons, soon fraying in a thousand ways with every slight breeze, then finally dispersing. When the air is still, the houses cast their forms and muted hues onto the rippling water, along with the loftier peak of the church.

Before continuing on his way, the traveler is urged to direct his gaze groundward: it is not unusual to find, by the side of the road, in the sandy gap separating the asphalt from the dense intricacies of the grass, several specimens of a sort of red ant to which, in this region, many a living tradition is linked.

The village's history is a hazy one, owing to a dearth of archival records, entirely destroyed, or nearly so, by a distant disaster, very likely a fire, in the days of the wars of religion. Another fine opportunity, then, for disputes on the subject of origins.

Bannière

Here, one bygone day, when the weekly market had filled the town square with farmers and villagers, amid livestock, food-stuffs, and diverse entertainments, the customary tumult—laughter, cries, disputations, whispers—suddenly waned. Silence. The sun had emerged from the clouds. Eight strangers stood at one corner of the square, shaking the dust from their tunics. One raised a banner embroidered with the emblematic cross, then planted its shaft in the gap separating four cobblestones. These instigators of the Crusade had come to awaken ardors and strike fear into the soul. Perhaps their orator spun out rousing descriptions contrasting the inferno's red flames with the delicate azures of paradise. No doubt he evoked the primordial rivalry of goods and evils, and how this subterranean struggle sometimes surfaces in the form of fierce battles, each one apparently decisive, in the heat of which any attempt at indifference equates to support for the opposite side.

The lavish phantasmagoria inscribed in every mind by these words left the audience shaken. Instantly the adolescents' passions were inflamed. Their elders—fathers or brothers—discreetly sought to distract them from the flag's snapping billows, amid which the cross, continually metamorphosing, seemed alternately to vanish and to be reborn. In vain: some had been contaminated, and already these efforts to curb the mounting inspirations swelling their breasts struck them as sacrilege. Several ran off at a breakneck pace, eager to snatch up some garment to

3

Bannière

prepare for the imminent departure; a number of others, their imaginations not nimble enough to call up the splendid Orient, were convinced indirectly, by the determination of family or friends. Few returned, or none. Between those households that had sacrificed some of their number and those that, by chance or prudence, had remained entire, muted rivalries arose, soon exacerbated by the subsequent new divisions of power and land. As the province's tortuous history wended onward, these conflicts continued to smolder, it seems, and sometimes on strangely petty grounds. Given the crucial role played by the recruiters' banner, its emblem alternately crushed and unfurled by the wind, the village was given the name that it bears to this day.

The other camp, as might be expected, puts forth an entirely contrary theory.

Several times destroyed and rebuilt, a victim of countless vicissitudes, the village church holds little interest today, save to situate the original edifice. It nevertheless reassembles, in a very different order, the sum of its forerunner's parts, and for this reason certain tourists find a secret charm in its walls, as if, imprisoned in the current monument, the earlier architecture might reveal itself to a sufficiently erudite gaze.

On the other hand, the traveler will be amply rewarded by a visit to a house on the town square, inhabited for seven or eight

Bannière

years at the turn of the century by one Albert Crucis. This latter had claimed the title of painter, and indeed—as the traveler might, if he wishes, verify for himself—the oils, watercolors, and drawings produced by his hand show a first-rate command of that craft. Nevertheless, though interested enough in the province to engage in frequent excursions and recurrent tête-à-têtes with the aged locals in the café, all evidence suggests that he never found full acceptance in these parts. The silence in which he veiled his past and the illness that compelled him to retire to these relative heights gave rise, in the community, to numerous hypotheses. Perhaps "Albert Crucis" was nothing more than a pseudonym; and so, false names being commonplace among artists, he began, late in life, to cultivate a talent of his youth, by way of justification. In hushed tones, some ascribed to him a criminal past, or (owing to his occasional visits from friends, hastily dubbed "envoys") revolutionary aspirations; others defended him. Some claimed the broad, sinuous scarf in whose folds he swaddled his neck, excessively announcing his illness, rendered its reality dubious. One evening, nevertheless, a team of medics spirited the invalid away, with a wealth of precautions. It was later learned that Albert Crucis had bequeathed to the village certain of his works, along with his house, in which the former would be gathered to constitute a museum.

The drawings and watercolors advantageously arranged on the

Bannière

walls of the ground floor's main room are notable for their extreme economy of line and of paint. Everywhere, it seems, the white of the paper has been assigned a predominant role. Hence the artist's marked preference for expanses lavishly covered in snow, for cloud-laden skies, and for reflections by which to duplicate such propitious scenes. This reading is contested, however, by the oil-paintings, where those same masses of snow and cloud are on the contrary obtained by thick layerings of white. A singular trait: on each of these works, the signature is ornamented by two fine lines, forming a cross, standing in for the dot on the *i*.

In accordance with the Master's instructions, several pieces—a vast oil painting and eight landscapes—have been consigned to a separate room on the upper story. Concerning these latter, if properly solicited, the guide will nonetheless provide certain insights.

"Given this canvas's lack of a title, which in some cases Albert Crucis did not hesitate to omit, might there exist some document that elucidates, however obliquely, the sense of this allegory?"

"Alas! Monsieur, it would appear not. Were he questioned on such a subject, the Master always replied, not unmysteriously, that the title was quite obviously inscribed on the paper or canvas. We did however discover, in his studio, a flag, which, despite

Bannière

the colors' inversion, seems to have served as a model for the scene on the far left; and for that reason we have raised it, on its staff, in the middle of the room. As you see, it is an ancient banner whose fringe and scarlet surface have, over time, been ravaged in various ways. Here you will find a rip, reverently restitched, and there, creating a complex arborescence, that dark stain. The white cross, better preserved, was no doubt sewn on at some later date. Note that the cross is composed of four isosceles triangles, their summits joined at the center. This is the emblem of the Knights of Malta. As you know, that religious order—the first born of the Crusades, since it dates back to 1099—was ruled by a grand master, and divided into nations, or tongues, numbering eight in all. Certain knights wore their white enamel cross around their necks, as a medallion.

"There is little likelihood that the oriflamme is authentic, even in part. In what circumstances Albert Crucis acquired it, no one knows. Nevertheless, some assert that this is indeed the notorious standard whose movements, one bygone day, on the square, distributed so many endlessly mutating figures. And this theory might give rise to another: that the painter chose to withdraw to a locale such as ours only in that the historical artifact of which he was the guardian prompted him to do so. No doubt such a notion adjoins an unthinkable frivolity to an excess of ingenuity. If you

Bannière

look closely at the left side of the canvas, you will in any case observe the similarity of motif and form aligning the present banner with the flag wielded by that stout man-at-arms."

Obeying the guide's injunction, the young visitor approaches the allegory, but his inspection is soon hampered by the shadow of his slightly tousled blond hair. He takes several steps back.

In the canvas's center, overlooking a dale obliquely shaded by the boughs of an oak tree shown on the left, a calvary raises its towering cross against the turbulent sky. To the left of the tree, at the summit of a distant rise, the walls and lofty towers of a fortified château can be made out. Finally, in the far left foreground, a helmeted soldier in a coat of mail clutches the banner's shaft with one hand. A breeze propels the fringe and the silk's mobile curves toward the right. Against its rippling white background, the red Maltese cross is affected in a manner easily read by the eye. The visitor draws ever nearer the canvas, in vain; his scrutiny seems to have left him disappointed. No doubt his head's shadow, once again cast onto the painting's surface, is concealing some tiny clue ...

"Perhaps, Monsieur, you were hoping to find, on the painted banner, some form duplicating the arborescent stain or the rip that disfigure the model?"

The traveler laughs:

Bannière

"With a painter as meticulous as this, nothing must be neglected."

"I do not doubt, Monsieur," adds the guide, "that, as was his wont, the Master would have responded, concerning such signs, that they could be found quite obviously inscribed on the canvas ... Elsewhere, perhaps, or further along."

Like several other villages in this region, Bannière abounds in picturesque sites, easily reached by a number of radiating footpaths. The Albert Crucis Museum, a visit to which is recommended, offers a rich anthology of such spots. To be sure, by pursuing his own itineraries, anyone might discover locales more favorable for pictural meditation. Convexities: every eminence overlooking an outstretched expanse below. Concavities: bends in the river, with a vault of branches inverting its arch in the current.

Often the traveler's eye is caught by the village's walls, even those of the humblest abodes. No doubt their simple beauty derives from the absence of mortar in their construction. Given the prohibition of any compound to compensate for their flaws, all commonplace stones are excluded. Everywhere the villagers have chosen fine rectangular parallelepipeds, flat of face, with well-defined corners. An edifice's erection is dictated by its preliminary cornerstones, alternately lending their length and their

9

Bannière

width to the two perpendicular walls. Again and again this offset figure recurs, in staggered rows, with only the most minimal variants caused by the tiny discrepancies of two neighboring stones. Approaching the wall almost to the point of touching it, one will discover a whole network of new spaces, endlessly varied, of microscopic dimension. Pitting yellow tones against oranges and mauves, all manner of mosses and lichens create splendid landscapes on the stones' surface, sketching out paths that one might sometimes wish could be followed toward more secret passageways.

But the two strident tones of a siren, suddenly erupting around that minuscule silence, put an end to the reverie.

"What's happening?"

"I believe it must be the police, Monsieur."

"An ambulance, I would have thought."

"Because of the red cross, Monsieur. On reflection, however, your hypothesis is not entirely unthinkable, for I understand that the police are seeking a dangerous madman, a pyromaniac, recently escaped from a psychiatric ward."

The right half of the canvas is simpler: neither walls nor soldiers, not a cross to be seen. Three hills alone, in the distance, form a massif. Along one slope, their vegetation, with several trees

Bannière

emerging from the anonymous greenery at the summit, is suffering the ravages of a wildfire.

Glowing red embers are strewn over the ground. Now and then arise columns of flame, undulating, soon eclipsed by the dark fumes they provoke. Thus emerges, with trunks of flame and boughs of smoke, the image—magnified, mobile, and final—of the obliterated forest.

Rising diagonally, the smoke pales, metamorphoses toward the left, and finally melds with the ponderous white tones of a thundercloud lurking in the skies. Below, between the cross and the blaze, lies an area already destroyed, with its ashes, its wisps of smoke, its charred branches.

There is thus, indisputably, a twofold contradiction. While the fire mounting the hillside is spreading left to right, the wind, as the smoke's drift reveals, is blowing in the opposite direction—and hence controverts, on the other end of the canvas, the moderate breeze rippling the flag rightward.

"In their profusion, would such anomalies not suffice to define this work as an allegory?"

"No doubt, Monsieur," the guide replies. "A similar hypothesis—and expressed in identical terms, if memory serves—was in fact put forward just now by a young person who inspected this display's every detail with a diligence at least equal to yours."

Bannière

"At least equal to mine, you say?"

"Indeed, Monsieur. Before this canvas, for example, she solicited my permission to draw up a succinct sketch."

"And you granted this wish?"

"Why, naturally, Monsieur. In his papers, the Master left no room for doubt: future admirers of his *oeuvre* were to be granted every possible license. Immediately the young lady pulled a white sheet from her portfolio and set to work. To my great surprise, I must admit, Monsieur, she fashioned not a figurative representation but a singular diagram, abounding in arrows and numerals, letters, even a few quick lines of commentary, immediately struck out with a most handsome pen-stroke . . ."

"And how long since she left?"

"She went on her way a few moments before you arrived, Monsieur."

"In red?"

"Dressed in red, do you mean, Monsieur?"

"Yes, of course."

"To be sure, Monsieur, she wore a rippling red dress, whose subtle elegance, may I say, I admired. In her hair, a bow echoed that same color. Perhaps you know this young person?"

"It's not out of the question."

Far to the right, on the undamaged flank of the hill, a short foaming line describes a cascade's course through the trees. Soon

Bannière

the flow vanishes, only to reappear in the foreground, resurgent. In that water, now stilled, are reflected, backward, in spite of a reverently restitched rip, the oak tree's dark arborescence and the calvary's cross.

The visitor approaches the window, almost to the point of touching it, and gazes briefly over the landscape before him. Neither distant citadel nor many-boughed tree; not a man-at-arms to be seen outside, between the wooden panels, today.

As a rule, no traveler worth his salt will let himself be entirely distracted by the hamlets, legends, and landscapes whose configurations are laid out in the present guidebook. Impromptu, even at the foot of a vast edifice or on a belvedere offering irreconcilable prospects, he is able to put into play events seemingly too fortuitous, or too minimal, to interest the common run of men.

One would, for instance, have to bend down, and perhaps even kneel at the edge of the sidewalk, to learn what will become, in the dust, of that assiduous ant. Several meters upstream, fed by some brutal artifice, a torrent is rushing over the rut of the gutter. Eddies, wavelets, mobile splashes of sunlight, whirling flotsam ... Its body half engaged in the gap separating four cobblestones, the insect, here, today, pursues its occupations. Bits of straw, foaming cascades, microscopic whitecaps, surging rapids, riptides, whirlpools. Must the visitor, after casting a wary eye over

Bannière

his surroundings, now come to the creature's aid? Urgently frighten it off with a blade of grass? Graze its body, imperceptibly, as a last resort, with one finger? Or rather, but no less attentively, maintain a state of perfect neutrality?

With the floodwaters' arrival, the ant has taken several steps back, and for the moment finds itself out of harm's way atop a rise on the rectangular stone. On either side, roaring and lapping, the water pours by. Indiscernibly the tide rises, modifying the dry area's outline. The water first attacks the corners of the original rectangle, rounding them off, soon creating an almost perfect ellipse. Here and there, nonetheless, a delay in the flow reveals an invisible incline on the stone. Now the ant scurries back and forth over the convex surface, too hurried for the details of its maneuvers to be understood. Having mounted continuously for some time, its agitation suddenly ebbs: henceforth, it seems, the insect will merely align its body with the axis of the greater of the islet's two dimensions. Should some happenstance disturb the stone's temporary contours, the ant immediately adjusts its position. It stands perfectly still. Its antennae alone, at the top of its head, remain vigorously active. The spectacle gives rise to a curious emotion, distant, as if ancestral, and demanding intervention. Should the visitor lower some leaf toward the ground? Allow the animal to embark and run hither and yon over the guidebook's pages? Or rather, on the pretext of shortening the animal's agony in that dark

Bannière

watery labyrinth, seize this occasion to commit, in miniature, a perfect murder? Perhaps, having determined its species, crush the imprisoned beast with one foot, slowly, pivoting slightly? If so, depending on the direction then taken, either the road or the sidewalk will afterwards bear, at fixed intervals, visibly fading, a damp print in the shape of a shoe.

Before moving on from this village, a certain traveler may desire a few final details concerning the doctrine that, on the pretext of poetry, infers things from words. In the case of the Damier, the dogma asserts that this name itself is an origin. Reflecting on the meager herbage produced by the area's pothole-riddled limestone, some devotee, long ago, certain that everything is ordered by language's edicts, must have imagined the following: since the river's waters go by the name "Damier," might not a vegetal checkerboard, interspersing woodlands and pastures, offer the best hope of conserving the ambient moisture?

As for the putative scene on the town square, in some dubious distant past, with those chaotic diversities, those noises, that stupor, the dust on the tunics, and the banner's red hues—so curiously common to Hell and the Cross—it is, this dogma tells us, pure fiction, derived from the village's name, previously conferred. And it is to this same process, some would say, that we must link the establishment, at the end of the last century, in a

Bannière

house by the side of the river, of a manufactory of flags and gonfalons. No doubt, by founding his enterprise on the sign of an emblematic red cross, the artisan hoped to draw from the town's name the precious idea of a longstanding tradition. But his business met with a grim fate. One night, flames appeared at the windows, and in the water. Spreading furiously, they left behind, after the collapse of the roof, only a charred mass of crenellated ruins. One extremist, touting his skill in the reading of texts and the study of canvases, blamed this disaster on the cross's flamboyant red hues, escaped from their geometric prison. To minimize his advantage, the other camp's sole solution, it seems, was to insinuate, not unmenacingly, that in his ardor he might well have lent them a hand.

We must also cite a surprising interpretation of Albert Crucis's work. Inscribed atop every signature in the guise of the dot on the *i*, the minuscule cross must possess, it is claimed, a pedagogical sense, to be read as follows: This is my name that I am depicting. Indeed, whether true name or alias, "Crucis" is simply the genitive of the Latin *crux*, "cross." This discovery might give rise to another: if, as a counterproof, we now turn to the name "Albert," we will observe its odd proximity to the Latin *albor*, designating a whiteness. Thus might be explained the painter's fondness, in all media, for the color white, and very likely, by extension, certain other phenomena too.

Beaufort

Whatever his motive for passing through Beaufort, whether originating in some mere caprice or conforming to the demands of a breakneck itinerary blindly traversing the province, whether stemming from some subtle calculation or more simply, today, from the name's seeming promise of ancient stone walls, no traveler can long remain unmoved by the curving perspective offered, from the main road, by the lane climbing up to the village. Should he take that turn, the crenellated trimming of the hedges to his right and left must not distract him from the thoroughfare's unusual nature. For that roadway, eschewing any change of direction, describes the rings of a spiral all around the hill, straight to the summit, where Beaufort-le-Haut stands. Better yet, the village's layout continues this figure, no less impeccably. Bordered by two rows of dwellings, the single street curls its way to the miniature plaza at the town's center, the endpoint of the ascent. Such a design has its drawbacks. The attentive visitor will find these lessened by four steep staircases, running through vaulted galleries beneath the town's houses, linking the plaza to each level of the spiral. Naturally, the utility of these shortcuts is clearest to those most familiar with the locale.

Beaufort

However well suited the setting, there is no château at Beaufort. Not a ruin to be seen, nor even a mere token vestige; no stretch of wall ornamented with crenellations by the fall of certain stones from the summit. We might readily surmise which camp will claim victory from this fact: if the hilltop has never been home to a fortress, does that not prove that a place name, even endowed with an evident meaning, by no means always translates an antecedent reality? Better yet: if we recall that the greenery on either side of the road has been trimmed to figure a series of crenellations, we must manifestly grant that it is rather the place, in the end, that obeys the name that defines it.

Such certitude little troubles the opposite camp. They observe the village's curious configuration; they note the single street, readily barricaded; they consider the solid construction and exceedingly narrow windows of the houses forming the spiral's outermost ring. From this they conclude that, the absence of fortifications notwithstanding, the settlement as a whole has all the semblance of a citadel. Thus, whatever the theses of a misguided doctrine, the origin of the name is the village itself, which, in its singular geometry, is well and truly *beau, fort*, and *haut*—beautiful, strong, and high.

Any traveler interested enough in this region to indulge, if not in the cumbersome craft that is painting, then at least in frequent ex-

Beaufort

cursions and recurring tête-à-têtes today with the aged locals in
the café, may well encounter certain intransigents, betrayed, despite their reserve, by the oddity, in the end, of their stories. By
their lights, it was no accident if various cities and towns in the
province saw their annals destroyed, long ago, in the days of the
doctrinal wars. No doubt certain documents of the highest importance were in this way reduced to cinders, after the flames had
sent a thousand anodyne pages crumbling, whole slabs at a time,
glowing red, into the ash heap.

Thus, notably, might have vanished the proof that a fortified
château had indeed once existed at the top of the hill, with its towers, its crenellations, its banners unfurling their blues and golds
against a pure azure sky with every faint breeze.

Below, all around, the enemy's army had set up its encir-
clement, confronting the convex walls with the perpetually evolv-
ing details of its own concave fortifications. The prohibition of entry was matched by an interdiction of egress. Nothing remained
of the skirmishes that had erupted along this curving boundary
over the previous few days, save various now-useless bits of debris—fragments of arrows and lances, crushed helmets, battered
shields, shreds of cloth—reassembled by the enemy in a new order, as crude tumuli, scattered here and there at the foot of the
ramparts.

The assailants had abandoned the ruinous tactic of surface at-

Beaufort

tacks. Henceforth, the siege's outcome would depend on the subterranean maneuvers of their engineering teams. Starting from
the corners of a square enclosing the edifice to be destroyed, these
men in red each day disappeared silently into the depths of the
earth, equipped with strange tools, their mission to dig four converging tunnels.

"If I might interrupt . . . Must it not be deduced, from the care and
conviction with which you report them, that you acknowledge
some accuracy in these unlikely legends?"

As if making a casual remark, the young man has not turned
toward the antiques dealer. He continues his tour of the gallery;
spying a broad mirror, he advances diagonally toward it, the
greater part of the shop offered up to his gaze in the depths of the
blue-tinged, gilt-framed glass. Inversion is visible in every detail.

Left-handed, now, is the suit of armor in the entryway, clutch-
ing an inclined staff.

Its flag, endowed by an invisible rod with the specious ability
to flutter toward the draft from the open door, now undulates in the
other direction.

Curiously traced in the form of a spiral and reversed on the
pane's inner surface, the window's red-painted inscription re-
gains its original order. The curling string of capital letters has
again become readable: EPSILON, ANTIQUARIAN.

Beaufort

The antiquarian too has changed roles: ardently eyeing the mace in his hand, he might well pass for a customer, fascinated by his find.

The reading of these metamorphoses seems to direct the young man's thoughts toward a different problem entirely. He begins to murmur:

"Might the contrary movements of banner and smoke in Crucis's allegory designate a mirror effect?"

But the shopkeeper replies:

"A delicate question indeed, Monsieur. May I be perfectly frank? I wonder if, beneath my apparently fanciful story, you have not intuitively found some subterranean coherence, and interpreted my stance on the basis of your own nascent interest. For my part, I derive too real a benefit from these tales to spin them solely for customer's pleasure."

"Do you take part in the strange quarrel that seeks to decide, between words and things, which is the primary force?"

"Not at all. The foundational presence of a château at Beaufort-le-Haut would no doubt favor the thesis of language as translation of a prior reality, but I little trouble myself with such questions. I am above all a merchant, Monsieur, specialized in the sale of medieval weapons. One can easily grasp how I might profit from the existence, long ago, in this spot, of that fabled edifice. Whether dating from that period or from a posterior age, whether authentic

Beaufort

or counterfeited on the instructions of some informed connoisseur, the objects that I display—these standards, these shields, these helmets, lances, and arrows—earn from that proximity a certain prestige. If only a little, and sometimes that is enough to elicit a sale, the visitor vaguely believes, despite my denials, that they come from the leveled château. But you don't appear to be listening . . ."

"That red car . . . Tell me, the staircase I spy on the other side of the street, ascending under a vaulted ceiling—is that one of the shortcuts by which the hilltop can be speedily gained?"

"It is, Monsieur, but . . ."

Nimbly dodging the weapons arrayed all through the shop, the visitor has rushed out the front door. He crosses the street. He slips into the dark passageway. Since, with every stride, each step beneath his feet proves uneven, endless jolts and surprises trouble his climb. He emerges onto the street, today, at the next level up: no sign of a car to his right, nor his left . . . Again he crosses. Into the passageway he slips. With every stride, each step, uneven. In the street, left, right, nothing. Dark passageway. Endless surprises. On the plaza, at the summit, still nothing, save the roundabout ringing the well that serves as a hub for the traffic's rotary course, denoted by three circling white arrows on a blue metal disk.

Beaufort

Hands in his pockets, the young man wanders back down the spiral, idly observing his form's successive duplications in the shop windows. From his doorstep, the antiquarian observes this approach, arms crossed.

"Clearly, our tunnels have done little to further your cause. Of course, had you been a bit more inclined to hear me out . . ."

"That car . . ."

"Precisely my point. I was about to remark that our village's spiral arrangement, of which I have made use to display my insignia on the shop window, forces every vehicle, after circling the plaza, to descend by the same route, in the opposite direction. I am in fact surprised, given that you were studying a mirror at the time, that the idea of an inversion never entered your mind. Rather than climbing those hazardous staircases, you would have done better simply to follow the street. Contrarily, on your return, you might best have taken the shortcut, so as to meet up with the vehicle, which was stopped further down . . ."

"Where?"

"Here, Monsieur. Disconcerted by your sudden departure, I stood for a moment on my threshold. I was returning to the back room when the slam of a car door, nearby, gave me a start. An elegant young woman had just climbed out of the auto you seemed to be chasing. She crossed the street, gazed at the ground for a moment, then advanced toward my window. She studied the interior

Beaufort

of my shop—most particularly, it seemed to me, the mirror you were contemplating when she first made her appearance. And then I made what may have been, I admit, a mistake. Supposing that this was the young person you were hoping to find, I rushed out to hail her, and invite her to await your return. Did she misread my intentions? Did she believe I was about to spontaneously tout some feature of my display? Immediately she turned on her heel and reboarded her car. She had just disappeared when I saw you returning, hands in your pockets, unhurried."

But this account seems to interest the young man far less than a series of damp shoe prints on the sidewalk before him.

"That," he says, pointing one foot toward the trail, visibly fading, "was her?"

"Yes, and as it happens the behavior of your . . . friend did not fail to surprise me. Approaching the sidewalk, she glanced toward the torrent rushing over the gutter with all manner of miniature whirlpools. An unexpected misstep sent her foot into the water—but only at the edge, I am happy to say, from which, unevenly, one cobblestone still emerged."

Still speaking, the antiquarian has returned to his shop, forcing the young man to follow in order to hear. Once again encircled by armaments, the latter concedes:

"Perhaps I shouldn't have stopped you? After all, however fan-

Beaufort

ciful some of its episodes, I was beginning, as you guessed, to discover a strange charm in your story. Can we not discern in that account the echo, even if muted, of some important event, gradually reshaped by many metamorphoses? Those engineers, you were saying, silently advancing into the depths of the earth, their mission to dig four converging tunnels . . ."

". . . finally realized their assigned task, if I might interrupt, after all manner of burrowing. Under the massive stone walls, they piled keg upon keg. They then laid down a ribbon of black powder in each of the four galleries. Since that inflammable dust blended in with the soil, they were obliged, as a first step, to inscribe a long red line on the ground. Too, so as to avoid any hiatus in the flame's propagation, they patiently skirted the tiny excrescences still studding the passageways' floors, in spite of their painstaking labors. These final precautions prolonged their task. But when, at the appointed hour, the signal was sounded—broadcast, in mocking paradox, by a delicate melody played on an oboe —and the powder was finally lit, their offensive went off without mishap.

"First, all around, with mounting amplitude, the earth began to tremble.

"A rumble rolled through the skies, and the citadel rose up, soon expanding in every direction; with all manner of fissures, it burst open, then scattered in the form of its constituent stones.

Beaufort

"Few survived, or none. So as to snuff out the enemy's ideology even into the future, it was decided that nothing would remain, not even a ruin. Rather than expend a vast sum removing the château's materials, they thought it more elegant to build with them, on the very site of the edifice, the first homes of a settlement. Thus, the village's geometric layout might be explained by its entirely arbitrary origin. No doubt, however, the four staircases, beneath their shadowy vaulting, form a surviving trace, intentional or no, of the galleries dug from the earth at the time of the siege."

"Or the sign of a cross. But what I find most striking," the young man remarks, "has evidently eluded you. It is true, as you told me, that you take little interest in questions of language; otherwise you would have observed that, already present at Bannière, in the church's construction, the exclusive use of one edifice's materials in order to obtain another is, indisputably, an allegory of the anagram. I am surprised that, with your knowledge of the province's legends, you failed to note this persistent principle, and above all that you never thought of applying it to your own name. For it is not difficult to discover that, differently ordered, the diverse letters of the name Epsilon, dear Monsieur, give us *l'Espion*: The spy."

Several of Beaufort's shops deserve more than an idle glance at one's own continually repeated image as one strolls past. The village's curious form attracts visitors in numbers sufficient to allow

Beaufort

the flourishing of many tasteful boutiques, evenly distributed on either side of the town's single street.

Sometimes brimming with lore from distant days, Beaufort's antiquarians delight in devising arresting arrangements for the display of their wares. Thus, in one shop, the visitor might admire, not without a burgeoning terror, how every weapon is ingeniously aimed toward one single point. Should a customer, sensitive to this insidious spatial arrangement, allow himself to be drawn toward the center of that convergence, he will there find himself menaced from every angle, in a thousand various ways. Better yet: the artist—for what other name can be given the creator of so potent a setting?—has placed at that spot a broad mirror, blue-tinged and gilt-framed. Might the cornered visitor seek some symbolic escape today, in those virtual depths so helpfully offered? If so, he will find on the other side not only the same weapons confronting him, but also his own face, ashen with alarm, and perhaps even, in the background, the antiquarian, who, the better to observe him, has picked up a rusting iron mace.

Though he knows full well he must one day part with his finds, every true antiquarian is at heart a collector, assigning himself—and requiring—specific criteria for the choice of the objects he sells. Thus, in Beaufort, where this trade has attained the loftiest heights, the traveler will discover all manner of specialists: furniture, lamps, curios, clothing and tapestries, prints and engrav-

Beaufort

ings, weapons and mirrors. Too, since the guild is close-knit, it has been ordained, at the chamber of commerce's behest, that each antiquarian must, by turns, mount a display centered on some distinct theme, its elements to be borrowed from his fellow merchants' stock.

Any traveler who studies the full array of shop windows will thus find, on the one hand, several series of similar pieces, and, on the other, diverse objects placed by their function in the scene on display. Need we add, today, that some controversialists, seizing every occasion to reignite their feud, have opted to read in this dual presentation a parable of the linguist's distinction between syntagm and paradigm?

These displays take a variety of forms. To give some idea of their nature, we will here simply detail the exhibit that caused, perhaps, the greatest stir. In this case, the penchant for analogy—characteristic of the collector's mind—appears to felicitously incorporate a diametrically opposed principle. To be sure, the display's premise forbade any assemblage of similar objects, whether weapons or curios, such as might be found in a private collection; might it nonetheless be possible to link the scene's diverse elements through some unifying resemblance? This idea took shape on the discovery, in two separate collections, of a tapestry in the Aubusson style and a little engraving from the eighteenth century, both representing the same piquant scene.

Beaufort

On the left-hand half of the paper, a profuse diversity of cross-hatchings suggested, in both form and contour, the rumples, the creases, the cascades of a canopy bed's sheets and curtains, at the far end of the room. Already close to the motionless turbulence of the linen and canvas, a man and a woman were half-struggling, entwined. Bent backward, the victim was endeavoring with her left hand to open the latch of the locked door, while her right, albeit with equivocal daintiness, pushed her assailant's torso away; meanwhile, the male was encircling her captive waist with his left arm, coolly closing the bolt with his right hand, and pressing his lips to the young woman's neck, causing her head to droop limply earthward, overcome with rapture. Four details—the well-tousled coiffure, a bared shoulder, the unbuttoned bodice, and the excessive dishevelment of the full skirt—rendered the scene entirely legible. After many ardent effusions of tenderness, betrayed by the bedclothes' disarray, the man, abruptly resolving to launch a decisive assault, had risen to check that the door was indeed locked. Seized by a sudden panic, his young friend, without troubling to straighten her clothing, had followed after, hoping to stop him ... Along with a broad mirror, duplicating the ambiguous foes, a print of indecipherable design completed the chamber's decor.

In contrast, the pose of the tapestry's figures was stamped with an almost ceremonious calm. In the background, an impeccable order ruled the curtains and sheets of a canopy bed. Her posture

Beaufort

erect, even somewhat stiff, eyes wide open, the lady stood facing the viewer, her right arm hanging at her side, her left hand abandoned to her lover's caresses. Seen in one-quarter profile, the gentleman was reverently kissing the left breast offered up by the carefully unbuttoned bodice. The lady bore four rows of eight pearls in her severely coiffed hair. A shared kinship with purple united the man's crimson garments with the blue of her dress, of the curtains, and of an indecipherable wall ornament.

To best display these images behind the shop's windowpane, no setting would do but a bedchamber in the style of days gone by, with a superb baldaquin bed. Dressed in period costume, two mannequins matched their poses and gestures to those of the decorative figures. In light of the bed's crimson silk curtains, there was no choice, if the tapestry was to be respected, but to reverse the clothing's hues. In a sumptuous, deep-cut crimson dress, the young lady sat on an invisible stool. Her black mane fell over her shoulders today; her face was raised, eyes questioning, toward the man, who, towering over her, gazed self-assuredly down. Perhaps she had just given him leave to draw near enough to place one hand on her left shoulder, and the other in her hair.

The entire scene was in any case easily imagined. Trusting, the girl had let herself be led into this room; but then, noting how closely the color of the bed's curtains matched her own dress, her

Beaufort

cheeks had begun to burn. The engraving, the tapestry, the bow and arrow affixed to the wall, the small heart-shaped table with a Dresden porcelain figurine of a gentleman kissing an elegant lady's hand, the strange figures ornamenting the rug, every element of the room's decor only added to her alarm. Approaching the blue-tinged, gilt-framed mirror, she discovered within it not the dimly imagined deliverance, but only those same troubling symbols, duplicated, and her own scarlet face. Her legs giving way, she collapsed onto a stool, eyes fixed on the man as he slowly advanced.

Despite certain anachronisms, this display proved such a rousing success that it was photographed for reproduction on polychrome postcards. An exemplar of that precious document may be readily obtained today from any bookdealer or souvenir shop in the region.

Belarbre

It is not uncommon to meet, in Belarbre, many travelers spotted earlier today beneath the vaults of Beaufort-le-Haut, in that town's single street. Some ten leagues from the touristic village, the road responds to the enticements of a nearby valley; soon it follows the bed of a narrow river, the Demoiselle, conforming to its every meander. A visitor willing to stop at the place called "le Tournant"—"the Turning"—may there witness a phenomenon rarely seen even in hilly calcareous regions such as this. Setting off from a bend in the road, a steep footpath will lead him, beneath a verdant arcade, straight to a place where the river's waters begin to whirl in a swift spiral.

If chance has not sent a fragment of bark, several leaves, or some manner of twig tumbling into the current, he need only gather such objects from his surroundings and cast them into the river at some point upstream. In so doing he will better distinguish the waters' rotations, made manifest by the flotsam: he will see the debris veer, then spin, and vanish into the center, aspirated by an intense circular flow. Whence it is proven that a part of the liquid

Belarbre

is diverted from the stream's major course, flowing on through some underground gallery, deep in the karst.

The insistent linguistic quarrel of which we have made ourselves the echo finds, in this site, the opportunity for a resurgence. Some contend that the aqueous eddy, indisputably prior, was, at a later time, endowed with the label "le Tournant." If their adversaries—albeit noting that the issue has not yet been fully explored—provisionally accept this interpretation, they do so only to better reveal another side of the question: how to explain the bend that, at this very spot, so strangely warps the path of the roadway, if not by granting that this turn was inspired by that selfsame name? While it is not our place to take sides in this polemic, every traveler must concede that no geographical feature here necessitated a curve. Better yet: it would appear that, with this premature change of direction, the road is forced to encounter several complications that it would otherwise have been spared: the crossing of the Demoiselle by means of a bridge, for example, and the comparatively arduous passage on the opposite bank, where sheer limestone outcroppings demand many a tunnel. Some, aiming to buttress their thesis, have gone so far as to sketch out the elegant course that the road might have taken were it not for this turn. So at least claim several admirers of Albert Crucis's painting, on permanent display in the city of Bannière. It is true that

Belarbre

one of the Master's canvases, depicting the Demoiselle's valley under a billowing mass of white clouds, includes, underscored by a regular alignment of trees, a certain wholly imaginary roadway.

Downstream, the landscape closes in: the Demoiselle slips into a narrow gorge, and the road undertakes many a daring, picturesque sinuosity alongside it. Emerging from the ravine, the current is broken by all sorts of cascades, prettily named "les Sauts de la Demoiselle"—"the Maiden's Leaps"—whose shimmering mists often seduced Albert Crucis's brush. A bit further along, beneath an arcade of branches, it meets a statelier river, the Dame, which figures among the Damier's affluents. If their junction enjoys a regular stream of visitors, it is because more than one arch tourist has been known to suggest, as a rather facile pleasantry, "Let's go see how the Demoiselle becomes a Dame!" In any case, the confluence is not without charm. The delicate ripples at the two currents' meeting ceaselessly stir up the reflected boughs, imparting a tremulous mobility.

Recent observations have revealed that the metamorphosis of Demoiselle into Dame actually takes place in a more secret spot. Noting that the Dame's source displays the carefree profusion characteristic of vauclusian springs, a team of geologists set out to discover the subterranean streams of which it formed the resurgence. Through frequent excursions and recurring tête-à-têtes

Belarbre

with the aged locals in the café, they catalogued every trickle that vanishes into a cleft, or imperceptibly wanes. In a Belcroix laboratory specialized in benzene derivatives, they located a ready supply of fluorescein, as required for their planned coloration procedure. Successively decanting this telltale liquid into several well-chosen springs, three times they saw the Dame's waters tinged, albeit subtly, with a fluorescent yellow. With this they moved on to a second experiment: they fed those three streams, meticulously timing the maneuver to be sure that the colored waters would reach the Dame's source at the same moment; but the resulting taint was far less pronounced than the first. Beckoned by fresh endeavors, they then went on their way. But soon it was realized that no one, strangely, had told them of "le Tournant." This liquid spiral was now colored in turn, and soon an intense fluorescence lit the Dame's rippling surface, suggesting that the water lost here was recaptured further on, after a change of name, by the same river. Some praised these works for having revealed various branches of the region's secret ramifying hydrography; others, knowingly, affirmed that the root of some deep symbolism had herewith been laid bare.

It may be best to decelerate in the outskirts of Belarbre, where no iron gate yet encloses the greenery, and perhaps even to stop at the edge of a vacant lot, not far from the child whose strange be-

Belarbre

havior has, in passing, been glimpsed. The gravel strewn over the sidewalk, then fragments of oddly fractured polished flint, grayish pebbles traversed by a vein, pieces of brick, and soon bits of rusted iron threaten, with any minuscule misstep, to betray the traveler's approach through the nettles. It soon becomes clear, however, that the child, one knee pressed to the ground, is too lost in his pursuits to hear a living soul. In one hand he clutches a magnifying glass of standard design: black handle, biconvex lens clasped in a metallic circumference. But far, it seems, from seeking an enlarged view of the pebbles and roots, of the soil, the grass, he is staring to one side of the instrument. His head, with its tousled black hair, is bent over the ground, where a tiny fragment of matter, its crystals somewhere between white and transparent, lies surrounded by a dense crowd of ants. These belong to a branch of the family said to be vanishing, small, bluish-black, with an imperceptible golden dot between their eyes. The swarm encircling the bait is continually crisscrossed by a mutable glow, its intensity varying inversely with its area. This brilliance is clearly produced by the magnifying glass, which, held at some distance from the objective, causes the sun's light and heat to converge at its focus. Whenever this beam, reduced to a perfectly incandescent pinpoint, lands on a fast-moving ant, the creature suddenly halts. When it sets off again, it walks with a labored, diagonal gait, still pursued by the harrying light, more expansive at

Belarbre

first, and less luminous, but soon recovering its most potent diameter. Soon the spotlit insect shrivels. A miniature sizzling ensues, with an odor of cooking flesh and a thin strand of smoke, soon ramifying, then dispersing into the air.

Whereupon, skillfully wielded, the lens can return to the moist sugar cube, and fresh prey.

"And what exactly are you up to?"

Roughly, the young man has seized the lad by his red sweater and forced him to rise, forearms raised fearfully over his face. After the initial tears, ineffectual and thus soon running dry, the child provides an account of the events, interspersed with sporadic hiccups. He was simply walking along the sidewalk, following the road, counting the trees perhaps, or, with one foot, randomly altering the gravel's perpetual disorder, creating a brief clatter amid the silence. No doubt he also gave a small hop from time to time. He kept his hands in his pockets. He spotted a car, red, gleaming, convertible, parked in the sunlight against the stone curb. Across the road, a few meters into the field, a young female, wielding a strange tool, was engaged in mysterious labors. He first threw a quick glance behind him. Fragments of oddly fractured polished flint, grayish pebbles traversed by a vein, pieces of brick, and soon bits of rusted iron threatened, with any minuscule misstep, to betray his approach through the nettles. It soon

Belarbre

became clear, however, that the young woman, one knee pressed to the ground, was too lost in her pursuits to hear a living soul. In one hand she clutched a magnifying glass of standard design: black handle, biconvex lens clasped in a metallic circumference. But far, it seems, from seeking an enlarged view of the pebbles and roots, of the soil, the grass, she was staring to one side of the instrument. Her head, with its silken black hair, was bent over the ground, where a tiny fragment of matter, its crystals somewhere between white and transparent, lay surrounded by a dense crowd of ants. These belonged to a branch of the family said to be vanishing, small, bluish-black, with an imperceptible golden dot between their eyes. The swarm encircling the bait was continually crisscrossed by a mutable glow, its intensity varying inversely with its area. This brilliance was clearly produced by the magnifying glass, which, held at some distance from the objective, caused the sun's light and heat to converge at its focus. Whenever this beam, reduced to a perfectly incandescent pinpoint, landed on a fast-moving ant, the creature suddenly halted. When it set off again, it walked with a labored, diagonal gait, still pursued by the harrying light, more expansive at first, and less luminous, but soon recovering its most potent diameter. Soon the spotlit insect shriveled. A miniature sizzling ensued, with an odor of cooking flesh and a thin strand of smoke, soon ramifying, then dispersing into the air.

Belarbre

Whereupon, skillfully wielded, the lens could return to the moist sugar cube, and fresh prey.

The better to enjoy this spectacle, he had approached; suddenly the young woman had started, startled, already on her feet, standing a full torso taller than he. She had called him back as he fled, her voice incomparably gentle, persuasive. Catching her breath, she had confessed to the alarm his unexpected presence had caused her, and soon launched into all sorts of abstruse explanations on the subject of something called focal length. Finally, placing the magnifying glass in his hand, she had shown him the strange use to which it could be put. With a smile, she had encouraged him to continue her labors. He had undertaken this task with such ardor, and soon with such profound joy, that he had forgotten the time, as well as the lady, who must have discreetly gone on her way.

"How long have you been at this?"

"I don't know."

"And how many ants have you set alight?"

"I don't know."

"Count them. Use the magnifying glass to help you see. Why are you fidgeting like that?"

"My right leg is asleep."

"You're afraid to say it, aren't you—you have ants in your

Belarbre

pants! Now, in another age, I have no doubt that you would have been tied up on the very scene of your crimes, naked, and smeared with a fine coating of honey. By their thousands, millions, and billions—for in those days their race must still have been flourishing—creating myriad arborescences around you, toward you, the ants would have advanced, shrouding your body from head to toe with their brisk pullulations."

"I count twenty-four, Monsieur, or twenty-three . . ."

"Which makes half an hour. As for you, do not suppose you will get off so easily. Your tingling leg has given me a solution."

And the young man pulls a number of nettle plants from the ground. He gathers them into a long bouquet, soon ravaging the leaves and stems with great blows against the child's thighs. As the patient yelps and squirms, clasped in an unyielding grip, the flagellation's first effects begin to appear, with rapid red welts and swellings spreading over the child's flesh.

"Understand that your victims have herewith found vengeance," the young man explains, grunting, in the midst of his efforts. "Understand that the urticating essence now penetrating your skin to wreak its caustic effect is nothing other than formic acid, to be found in the humblest ant."

All this notwithstanding, the city of Belarbre offers the traveler no curiosity so enticing as those of Beaufort-le-Haut. Far from it: un-

Belarbre

less compelled by some specific business, its visitors would no doubt be few if the town did not lie today on the road to Belcroix.

Unable to vaunt the lush foliage of some venerable durmast from which it might take its name, Belarbre lavishes particular care on the greenery of its outskirts. Thus, wherever generations of skillful pruning might allow it, the double arch of the plane trees lining the roads has been transformed into one single vault. Closely aligned with the grafter's art, this procedure's details can be summarized as follows. Two complementary incisions are first made in the boughs of two facing trees; the two branches are then joined, and secured by the coils of a ligature. With the two specimens thus wedded, the vessels of the wood and phloem instate a new, shared circulation. And if it is true that the branches' every ramification is matched, in strange symmetry, by an equal bifurcation of the roots, we might well suppose that, below ground, an irresistible tropism works to join the corresponding radices, and unite them. It is thus not without some mental pleasure that we might picture the town's outlying thoroughfares, running through the impeccable vegetal tunnels formed by the fusing of branches and roots.

The town's traditional concern for its greenery was further displayed, some years ago, by its relentless pursuit of a vandal despoiling the trunks of these trees. Purely by chance did this singular affair come to light. A certain botanically informed stroller,

Belarbre

often prompted by idle curiosity to study the desquamations of the plane trees close by his lodgings, one day found certain patches of bark affixed to a trunk with a suspect adherence. On closer inspection he observed, at the woody scales' edges, traces of some form of liquid, coagulated. Adroitly slipping a blade into the gap, he lifted the squama and sent it tumbling to earth. In its former location he found, not an underlying pale-yellow replica of its outline, but rather a surface hazed with a thick coating of glue, and most significantly a square window, hermetically sealed by a wooden panel one centimeter on each side. Dislodging this covering, he extracted, not without difficulty, a tiny cellophane envelope. In it lay the body of a red ant, of a species that flourishes in these parts. Finding several similar tombs on other plane trees nearby, he informed his friends of these findings, and soon the matter was raised before the town council. The initial indignation was tempered by the thought that this strange vandalism was likely mere schoolchildren's handiwork, of no real consequence. "Let us each recall our own childhood," one city father warmly intoned, "and the mysterious ritual battles, tortures, and burials that came with it—often not without pleasure." It was nevertheless decided that an inquiry was in order.

Untenable, soon, proved this deed's attribution to the hand of a child: every tomb had been carved at a height ranging from one

Belarbre

meter sixty to one meter seventy above the ground. Someone—
the town councilman, still clinging to his hypothesis—nonetheless insisted that, with one providing the other a boost, two boys
could well have performed these lofty labors. The inquest was
floundering, and this latter interpretation, taking root in the minds
of the undecided, began to gain some currency; but just then an
anonymous letter enabled, at long last, the culprit's arrest. The
message was not handwritten, but formed of cut-out bits of type,
so clumsily affixed to a leaf of paper that a smear of dried glue
emerged from under each character. Its external form notwithstanding, the accusation could scarcely have been clearer: "The
ants' assassin is old man La Fourmi." The nickname "La Fourmi"
—"the Ant"—had been conferred on a local park watchman,
fallen into vagrancy in the most pathetic of circumstances. Shortly
before his retirement, the old man had published, at his own ex-
pense and under a pseudonym both transparent and absurd, a
treatise assembling his strange notes on the behavior of ants, evidently jotted down in the public garden. Unconfirmed by a hasty
subsequent investigation, these findings, like the conclusions the
old man had drawn from them, were of a nature so utterly fictive
that they garnered only scornful hilarity from the townspeople. To
be sure, a few scattered souls ventured to defend the aged watchman today, but they proved powerless to shake the majority's
confidence. Deeply wounded by this mockery, the guard tendered

Belarbre

his resignation. This was his last dignified act: once unfailingly punctual and temperate, he soon fell into alcoholism and beggary. Here and there, now jeered by unruly children, now, contrarily, giving frantic chase, he could be seen roaming the vacant lots of the outskirts, among the nettles, muttering incoherent words, such as "And so they find vengeance, and so they find vengeance," confirming his pitiful state.

The anonymous missive had insinuated that the guard was not harmless. As he lay slumbering among the fragments of oddly fractured polished flint, the grayish pebbles traversed by a vein, the pieces of brick and bits of rusted iron, it proved simple to discover, in his ancient blue greatcoat, the knife, tube of glue, and sheet of cellophane that sufficed to indict him. Roughly awoken, he feigned incomprehension, and soon limited himself to a muted repetition of the words, "And so they find vengeance, and so they find vengeance."

A tragic development brought this affair to a close. As preparations were being made for his transferal to the Belcroix asylum, La Fourmi was temporarily housed in a cell at the police station, where he succeeded in ingesting the contents of a flask of insecticide. In his agony, his broken rant turned to a new theme. Steadfastly refusing to provide any fresh revelation, he endlessly murmured, until his last moment, "The Garden of Oppositions, The Garden of Oppositions, The Garden of O . . ." Such was his trea-

Belarbre

tise's title, and such was his name for Lenpois Park, of which he had once been the guardian.

Still holding to his hypothesis, the councilman who had put these events down to disorderly children now asserted that the watchman's tragic suicide did not, in theory at least, settle the case. To be sure, a not incoherent motive could be found for this vandalism, conjoining the two major branches of La Fourmi's life: on the one hand a preoccupation with insects, and on the other a disgraced park watchman's vengeance on the trees of the city. Not to be neglected, however, was the antagonism that seemed to govern his relations with the neighborhood youth. Would it not have been troublingly simple, as the old man lay slumbering, to slip the terrible proof of his guilt into his overcoat pocket? Too, the inquest had perhaps insufficiently emphasized that the anonymous letter's characters had, in an act of singular artfulness, been cut from the tract penned by the victim himself. To this came the retort that such finesse seemed rather at odds with the minds of the unruly children in question. In the end, since this polemic seemed apt to distract the populace from more crucial questions in the coming electoral season, and likely to be attributed to some machination of the opposing camp, it seemed preferable to pronounce the matter closed.

Lenpois Park lines the iron fences enclosing its lush verdure

Belarbre

with a boxwood hedge of such height that it is only on tiptoe, to-day, that a glimpse might be caught of the young woman in red slowly strolling the pathways, gesturing oddly.

Her gaze remains fixed on the ground, as if following, at the edge of the path, where the sand's irremediable disorder meets the dense intricacies of the grass, the shadows of her hands, now joined, now suddenly apart.

Sometimes, after a quick glance around her, she bends down and carefully studies the ground.

Then she stands upright, resuming her operations a bit further along.

The young man directs his steps toward the park's nearest entrance, several times peering over the hedge to check that the young female is not preparing to leave. Soon, a smile on his lips, he advances toward her, and, before she has raised her eyes, he asks:

"Is it for my benefit that you those strange signals?"

"No, of course not," she replies, with a start.

"That's a pity; I like nothing more than deciphering signs. My name is Lasius, Olivier Lasius."

"And I

Belcroix

am Atta. Sorry to disappoint you, but I was simply, as I strolled these magnificent pathways, casting various shadow forms on the ground, my thoughts elsewhere."

"And what is your repertoire?"

"A cat, a goat, a dog, a swan . . ."

"Would you show me? Oh! Very good; do you know many others?" asks the young man.

"No. Only an elephant, a rabbit, a fly, a fish. You know," she adds with a laugh, "I'm no expert in ombromania . . . And you?"

"Nor am I, but if we pooled our knowledge, no doubt we could each double our skill."

"Very well," she says. "I'll gladly learn whatever I might."

Whereupon, unhurried, the young man takes the black-handled magnifying glass from his pocket; laughing in turn, he replies:

"Perhaps you should use this, the better to see the flaws . . ."

"Where did you find that instrument?"

"Why? Does it seem familiar?"

"Perhaps, Olivier," Atta replies, another smile slowly forming on her lips.

Belcroix

"We shall see," says Lasius. "In the meantime, watch."

"It's a flag, followed by the head of an ant . . ."

"And this?"

"A cross, then a tree, leafless, its branches bare. It's winter-time, or else the tree is dead . . ."

"Owing, perhaps, to the ravages wrought on its trunk. And now?"

"A castle tower, with its crenellations, soon becoming, becoming . . . a profile, a man's profile, with an aquiline nose, and a peaked cap. A policeman, perhaps?"

"Or a park watchman—that one over there, shall we say, now head-on, observing us with such stern disapproval. Suggesting," adds Olivier today, "that we might do well to continue our chat in some more suitable spot. Perhaps, if you would, at the Café du Parc, where we will find not only a more tranquil setting but also, by way of its name, a means of prolonging our stay here a bit longer."

Having ordered a glass of tomato juice, Atta studies her hands, with boundless patience, as they lie flat on the Formica tabletop. She now seems little inclined to speak. Raising her fingers and their long red nails from the table, however slightly, would mean having to interpret the shadow they form. And given the two sources of light, the resulting figure would be one particularly re-

Belcroix

sistant to mastery: two separate shadows, producing, in their intersection, a still darker area. No doubt the reflected palm and digits would also come into play, imposing their various complications on the ensemble. But Lasius, idly toying with the magnifying glass, resumes the dialogue:

"It was turned over to me by a local child, not long ago, at the side of the road."

"Really? A gift, then?"

"Not exactly. He was engaged in a strange occupation, apparently fascinating, and I asked him to reveal his motive."

"And what was he doing?"

"Holding the instrument at arm's length before him, he was raptly admiring the minuscule landscape upside-down in the glass."

"Indeed, it was I who taught him that . . ."

"Now and then he drew the glass nearer, trying to make out how this capsizing of the world was achieved. Is it not a remarkable sight?" adds Lasius, gazing toward the distant lens in his turn. "Those inverted tables, and that tiny man in his white jacket, head down, perhaps bringing us our diminutive drinks?"

With flawless dexterity, the waiter sets the mint water before Atta and serves Olivier the tomato juice. The young man reverses the colored cylinders, and sententiously declares:

"We have entered the realm of exchange: first our shadow

Belcroix

figures, then our recent memories, and now our refreshments. Red suits you so well . . ."

"Better than green suits you, I should say!"

"Nothing laughable in my choice: red and green are complementary colors . . . At any rate, the child confessed that the object was not his, and that he wanted it returned to a woman in red, in a red car. I assured him I would see to it . . ."

"Well, really!"

"Have I not accomplished my mission?"

"That is not what surprises me so. Rather, it is the child's about-face, and his curious aptitude for lies. Judge for yourself. As I was driving at high speed through the outskirts, my thoughts were invaded by a marginal sign, mobile and insistent: a Maltese cross, formed of four isosceles triangles joined at their summits. I slowed down, and, beside a vacant lot, I stopped. At a height of one meter sixty or seventy above the ground, an isosceles triangle, point down, had been slashed into the trunk of the nearest tree. The next trunk bore the same sign, inverted. On the succeeding plane trees, the triangle could be seen with its point to the right, then the left. And so on . . ."

"You do realize," Lasius says, "that you were on the Avenue de Belcroix?"

"Yes, and what of it?"

Belcroix

"All signs suggest that these triangles, whose superimposition, at high speed, fashions a cross, were produced by some fanatical devotee of the theory that our universe is founded in language: the name 'Belcroix' gives rise to crosses. But what about the child, Atta?"

"Having brought into play the magnifying glass you are now holding, the better to study the tree's scars, I sensed a presence on my right, mute, motionless, and unexpected: the child in question, I suppose. His stance suggested so lively an interest in my acts that I could not help but show him the instrument and its strange ability, in certain cases, to turn the world upside down. Once he had the object in his hands, he immediately ran off at full speed, through the nettles, into the vacant lot, his precipitous footfalls upsetting the disorder of the pebbles and fragments of iron today."

"Why should he not have changed his mind or lied—several times, perhaps—once he had got hold of this reversing device? In any case, the time has come to make good on my promise and return to you so useful an object. I must nevertheless confess that such was not exactly the aim of my quest."

"Really? And what, my dear Olivier, was your mission's true goal?"

"Your car. I had arrived at the first dwellings, still sparse, of Belarbre, when my automobile suddenly veered to one side. From

Belcroix

the front left-hand tire I pulled a nail, deeply embedded; I then discovered, in the rear right-hand tire, two more . . ."

"The work of your fanatics, no doubt?" Atta remarks with a smile. "In the Avenue de Belcroix, the three nails of the Cross."

"Nails had been strewn over the pavement for a distance of several meters; most of them I removed. Then, as I continued toward the town center on foot, supposing that the neighborhood children were perhaps not uninvolved in this affair, I encountered the youth we both know. My first thought was to swiftly empty his pockets, but the game in which he was engaged, and the confidences he offered me, soon altered my plans. If only I could find the red motorist, I said to myself, perhaps I might persuade her to drive me . . ."

"Where?"

"To Cendrier."

"Your calculations were almost correct, dear Olivier, and no doubt would have been so entirely, were I not obliged, before continuing on to that town, to make a preliminary stop, of uncertain duration, in Belcroix. That's already half the way there, or almost. I'll take you. Come with me."

Even as she pilots the vehicle, the young woman's hands indulge in a supplementary activity: her fingers, and sometimes her pointed nails, hammer the amber circumference with small blows.

Belcroix

But if, before an oncoming intersection, a change of gears is required, we might admire with what authority her gestures, automatic and certain, forbid such small whimsies. As, on either side of the road, behind the trees, the houses grow ever sparser today, the needle on the speedometer wavers between seventy and eighty.

"Say, don't run over that old man trying to cross the avenue! How fast might that be in kilometers, incidentally?"

"Around one hundred twenty, I think," murmurs Atta.

"It's a shame," Olivier adds with a sigh, "that such speed requires so painful a restriction of the available space."

Whereupon, by various maneuvers, the young man seeks a more comfortable position. Finally he lifts his right arm and places it, cautiously, on his neighbor's seat back. The visitor will note that his hand immediately encounters a lock of black hair, minimally mobile. Idly closing together, the index and middle finger imprison the dark tress. Soon, with minuscule motions, the other fingers join in. The girl raises her eyes to the rearview mirror and asks Olivier if he might like a cigarette. He accepts.

"I believe you'll find them in there," says Atta.

With a brisk nod, immediately wrenching her hair from the fingers' grasp, she shows him the open glove compartment to the left of the speedometer. While his other hand strives to reestablish its bond with the lock of black hair, succeeds, moves on to the

Belcroix

right shoulder, and there engages in diverse limited wanderings, Lasius inspects the disorderly cache beneath the windshield. Thus, in succession, his left hand encounters a glove, the handle of the magnifying glass today, a comb, a red, white-lined handkerchief, a leaflet, for the moment illegible, the filmy tangle of a nylon stocking, a glove, the handle of the magnifying glass today, the leaflet, for the moment illegible, the comb, the red, white-lined handkerchief, the filmy tangle of the nylon stocking, a glove today, a black pouch, its cover snapped shut, a glove, the red, white-lined handkerchief, a glove, the black pouch, its cover snapped shut, the leaflet, for the moment illegible, a glove, the handle of the magnifying glass, the filmy tangle of the nylon stocking, the comb, a glove, the black pouch . . .

"Suppose you try using your other hand," says Atta.

"Very well, but first slow down."

"Now stop."

As his right hand, abandoning the shoulder, moves to the young female's face and turns it toward his, Lasius presses his mouth to her lips, first closed, then imperceptibly opening. Meanwhile, with all sorts of meanders and flourishes, his left hand slips down the neck, then over the bust, now violently and irregularly heaving, travels the length of the arm, the thigh, until it reaches the bend of the leg . . .

Belcroix

Suddenly Atta pulls away:

"Your other hand, Olivier, was for finding the cigarettes."

She smiles. She laughs. The attentive traveler will then note that she clasps the young man's head in her hands, and kisses him in her turn.

"Listen," she says, "if you don't object to a few hours' wait, we can go on to Cendrier together."

"I believe Belcroix has offered me its secrets already. I've no intention of wandering, without motivation, at the mercy of every spectacle, random and minuscule, that might hold me back . . ."

"Then your travels are guided by some precise goal?"

"Yes and no. I am searching, but I know not yet for what. Truth to tell," adds Olivier, "it's a very long story, dating back, it would seem, to the early days of this century, and the meeting in Belarbre's park of an adolescent and a certain strange personage, evidently a painter by calling. And from this, perhaps, you will understand why, hoping to meet you today, I obeyed the strange impulse beckoning me toward that selfsame park. The young man was Christophe Lasius, later to become my father. As for the painter, he signed his works Albert Crucis. Oblique on an easel where two pathways met, his canvas sat half-finished. But even now the young man was struck by the overly whitened sky, as by the slight liberties the artist had taken in his rendering of the

Belcroix

paths, the greenery, the flowerbeds. Rather than reproduce the present park, these assembled distortions, once grasped, seemed on the contrary to denote some urgent motif, necessary and enigmatic. It was then that the young man surprised the painter in a strange occupation: some distance away, one knee pressed to the ground, he was using a stout, black-handled magnifying glass to study the sandy zone adjoining the dense intricacies of the grass.

"A remarkable detail: he was stopped at the very spot where his canvas displayed several flowers absent from the lawn itself, red, whose stems, some leaning leftward, others right, produced an evident crisscrossing pattern. Perhaps sensing that his work and his person were being observed, the painter rose, strode back to the easel, as if counting his steps, and spoke:

'Perhaps you have questions, young man?'

'Several, Monsieur. Above all, I wonder what might be gained from this microscopic scrutiny of your model, given the little heed you pay the landscape, even going so far as to add this clutch of unexpected flowers to your canvas's lawn.'

"Crucis replied:

'Not quite so unexpected, these flowers, as you may think. No doubt this is difficult to grasp at first sight; but allow me to explain how far your exegesis of my acts, however logical, strays from the truth. To be sure, thanks to its dual optical capacities, the magni-

Belcroix

fying glass plays a crucial role in this affair. Its message, to be read
both literally (see the world more clearly) and figuratively (and
above all don't be afraid to turn it upside down) has for me, it is
true, an emblematic force. In the practice of my art, however, this
instrument allows me not to scrutinize an apparent model down
to the level of the invisible, but rather to verify on the canvas, oc-
casionally, the precision of this brush. In truth, I entered the
space defined by my painting only to check that the spot to which
I had added these crossed flowers did indeed, as it must, lie eight
meters distant from my easel. But there, the startling urge to examine the peculiarities of the ground took imperious root in my
mind.'

'That, at least,' the young man interrupted, 'I can readily understand. I myself, only a few minutes ago, experienced, as if
obeying some vital scenario, an unwonted desire to pass through
this park.'

'Perfect ... I thus took the magnifying glass from my pocket
and brought it into position, whereupon, inside the transparent
circle, I beheld a curious sight. A gigantic ant, red of body and
black of legs, was battling several specimens of the weaker blue
race, currently vanishing. Although fighting unaided, its superior
size and vigor offered the greater ant victory time after time.
Around it lay several tiny assailants, already maimed. Despite the
occasional influx of reinforcements, I little doubted this brawl's

Belcroix

outcome; but then I perceived, amid that mobile confusion, the contours of an underlying order.'

'Though often diverging to rescue some comrade in danger, the assailants were gradually driving the fight toward the shadow cast on the ground by several blades of grass, imperceptibly trembling. And then, all at once, an astounding development: no sooner had the giant insect entered the shade, in pursuit of its prey, than the battle's character was reversed. Along with these curious turnabouts, the traveler will note the delicacy of the shadows inscribed on the sands' minute disorder by the neighboring lawn. Suddenly the huge fighter's movements were marked by an unexpected torpor. And since, contrarily, its tiny opponents seemed invested with a new vitality, the beast was promptly brought to its knees, and severed into its constituent parts. It was then that I saw you studying my canvas. Perhaps you would care to visit the site of these operations?'

"Taking the adolescent by his elbow, the painter once again counted his strides, knelt, and in a voice hoarse with astonishment, murmured:

'There's nothing left—not the slightest trace. The light and shadow themselves have disappeared.'

'Because the sky, little by little, above us, look, has come to resemble its image in your painting.'

Belcroix

"Then, as if to himself, surprising the young man, who could not grasp what exactly this signified, Albert Crucis murmured:

'That's very good, very good indeed.'

"Whereupon, guiding him back toward the easel, he made a vague gesture that seemed to encompass both canvas and landscape:

'For all this, my dear boy, is nothing but metaphors . . .'

"Such was their first meeting; and, if I may believe the enigmatic allusions in my father's papers, Crucis's hold on the young man only grew stronger from that moment on."

"Did your father himself ever speak to you of all this?"

"My father never spoke to me at all, so to speak. Until his death, which came in my eighth year, he addressed me only in anodyne letters, for my education was entirely confined to a boarding school. I spent my vacations with a distant aunt, who, eight months ago, on my twenty-fourth birthday, entrusted to me a suitcase containing a disordered sheaf of papers.

"Now, at that time, I had chosen a subject for my history thesis, and was beginning to gather materials that might help me establish the importance of certain extremist cells, more or less aligned with the movement that provoked the upheavals of 1917. In such circumstances, Crucis's enigmatic behavior immediately caught my attention. His library, now lost, and, say my papers, so con-

Belcroix

spicuously abundant in studies of history and zoology, particularly dealing with ants, seditions, and the Crusades; his very visible activity as a painter, which brought him to diverse locales throughout the province; his glaring silence where his past was concerned; the vast scarf that he wore crossed over his breast: might all this, excessively touting his eccentric ways, not have served as a cover for secret revolutionary activities? And might not his frequent visitors, their speech often perceptibly accented, have been exiles, such as, aided by a network of contacts, frequently crisscrossed the continent to join in mysterious congresses? According to rumor, as confirmed by the excellent guide to this region, more than one of his Bannière neighbors was alarmed by Crucis's doings. Not entirely reassuring was the discreet speed with which he was one night spirited away, in an automobile emblazoned with a red cross. And so, leaving aside the metaphorical paternal notes, I resolved to devote my vacation to a brief inquiry. I supposed that a visit to the Bannière museum would bring me some insight, and I was not disappointed. A room on the upper floor, where, as per the Master's last wishes, several canvases have been placed on display, revealed an unmistakable itinerary. It passed through Belcroix, but a postcard, opportunely discovered en route, has allowed me to dispense with that stop. There thus remains, today if possible, the discovery of Cendrier. And you?"

Cendrier

"More than once, at first," Atta replies, "I felt I must interrupt you, to remark that your story coincided too often with my concerns not to have been derived, in its slightest details, from my own research. But each time I was held back, my suspicions subdued, by the antithetical notion that, embarked as we were on such parallel studies, only a miracle could have prevented our meeting, one day or another, here or there. And I would rather believe that it is our common project that has intuitively led us, with so natural a force, to come together, and that compels me, even now . . ."

As her left hand, abandoning the shoulder, moves to the young man's face and turns it toward hers, Atta presses her mouth to his lips, first closed, then imperceptibly opening. Meanwhile, with all sorts of meanders and flourishes, her right hand slips down the neck, then over the bust, now violently and irregularly heaving, travels the length of the arm, the thigh, until it reaches the bend of the leg . . .

Lasius abruptly pulls away:

"Your hands, Atta, are for driving."

He smiles. He laughs. The attentive traveler will then note that

Cendrier

he clasps the young woman's head in his hands, and kisses her in turn.

"Listen," she says, "if you have no objection to a few minutes' wait, I will tell you my story. But first you should offer me a cigarette, now that you've found them."

No sooner is it presented between the traveler's fingers, beneath the clouded skies, than a glistening appears on the cigarette pack below. This container takes the form of a rectangular red parallelepiped, tightly girdled in cellophane. Its accompanying letters and figures are printed in white. Without losing himself too entirely in their study, the visitor will successively read the words *Pall* and *Mall*, and then, between quotation marks, *Wherever Particular People Congregate*. At the top and bottom—if, on the basis of the printed words, we accept such an orientation—the pack is encircled by a narrow white belt. The lower band, directly inscribed onto the red packaging, seems to serve solely as a counterpart to the upper, a thin strip that must be detached from the cellophane to open the transparent wrapper. With this operation completed, the traveler will discover beneath it, printed onto the red packet, another white line, whose role is to act as a counterpart to the lower stripe. While the significance of this symmetry must not be neglected, let us rather examine, today, the central coat of arms.

On either side of an oval crest topped by a left-facing crowned helmet, two identically crowned lions stand facing each other, the

Cendrier

crest clasped in their claws. Symmetrically, the one creature's left side is juxtaposed with the other beast's right. Their lower limbs rest atop this motto, unfurled on an undulating length of fabric: "In hoc signo vinces"—"by this sign you will triumph." Shortly before a decisive battle, the story goes, a cross appeared in the heavens above Constantine's army, accompanied by these same four words. Promptly, it is said, he had this sign inscribed on his standard, and victory was soon his.

The traveler who grants this emblem sufficient attention will find several differences troubling the symmetrical sameness of the crest's twin bearers. More massive than its vis-à-vis, the beast on the right drapes a far fuller mane over its shoulders. Indeed, heraldic idealization notwithstanding, all evidence suggests that the creature on the left is no lioness: its pointed ear would seem to indicate some other species, perhaps that of the panther. We might thus wonder if, rather than displaying the central crest, the two fierce partners are not in fact struggling to snatch it away from each other. In this contest, the visible superiority of the beast on the right is seemingly counterbalanced by the success of the left-hand creature, toward which the helmet is gazing. Nor must we forget that, for convenience's sake, this portrayal reverses a coat of arms' traditional orientation. For in fact heraldry supposes, as is only natural, that the viewpoint is situated behind the crest. It is thus recommended to read *dexter* for left, and, for right, *sinister*.

Cendrier

The oval crest is itself ringed with the elliptical formula *Per aspera ad astra*: "Toward the stars, through difficulties." A cross divides the crest into quarters, identically paired on the diagonal. Here we see opposed, in various configurations, three lions, one atop the other, and a tower.

Before moving on from this emblem, a certain traveler may desire a few final details concerning the symbolic expression here enacted. No doubt he has already noted that each of the four inscriptions is composed of four words: *Pall Mall Famous Cigarettes*, *Wherever Particular People Congregate*, *In hoc signo vinces*, *Per aspera ad astra*. Too, it must be observed that the crest's four quarters display a total of eight signs: three lions and a tower, a tower and three lions. A count of the letters confirms this dependence on multiples of eight: the two Latin inscriptions comprise sixteen characters each, while the first of the two English legends employs twenty-four. Better yet: although we might expect to find thirty-two letters in the longer device, there are in fact thirty-four. This infraction can be easily read: neither more nor less than two in number, the added characters direct our attention back to the two heraldic figures on the verge of a duel. The whole thus depicts a brutal conflict in the offing, under the unvarying sign of the number eight. The sub-multiple four further designates the idea of a square: thus, there is thus every reason to believe that this battle makes use of eight squared, or sixty-four.

Cendrier

Olivier unwraps the pack. Flicking the base with one finger, he causes several long cigarettes to emerge, at varying lengths.

"Here you are," he says. "Soon to be reduced to ashes."

Atta replies:

"But first, it must be properly lit."

Whereupon Olivier strikes a match today and raises it toward Atta's face, trembling slightly. An incandescence appears at the cigarette's tip. Curling and billowing under the effect of their speech, the smoke and its honeyed aroma spread through the car.

"I believe my story dates back just as far as yours. There is a certain familial kinship between Crucis and myself."

"How could that be?"

"He is a fairly distant relation, I grant you: my grandmother's sister wedded him at the end of the last century."

"And what became of her?"

"She died not long after the wedding—horrifically, it would seem. Already with child, she was taking a rest holiday in Malta, delighting in long, solitary strolls amid the pines. One day, beneath a blazing sun, she was caught unawares by a raging wildfire, and soon perished, burned alive. Grief-stricken, Crucis had her ashes collected in an urn; learning from some thoughtless soul that such fires were sometimes caused by fragments of glass, adroitly laid out in the sunlight by ants so as to lay waste to their enemies' colonies, he embarked on a curious historical and zoo-

Cendrier

logical study. Could it be that this legend, devised and maintained by Crucis himself, served primarily to provide cover for his singular research? Once doubt raises its head, it can lead, with its irrepressible logic, to the most extreme of conclusions: some went so far as to claim that Crucis might not have been uninvolved in this most unlikely of deaths."

"Was Crucis his real name?"

"Very likely it was, but such was the suspicion he aroused that he inspired a favorite game in my family, whose rules can be summarized as follows: having discovered an anagram of the patronym Crucis, propose an interpretation that might motivate it. Among the more glittering triumphs, we might cite this solution: since 'Crucis' is the genitive of the Latin *crux*, it should be read 'Delacroix,' which etymology might reveal the source of the painter's vocation. Another proposed the anagram 'Cicrus,' to be understood as *sic russe*—'literally Russian'—and there found the root cause of the more or less revolutionary activities of which my great-uncle, as you know better than anyone, was suspected. Yet another, as I recall, suggested 'Circus,' seeking to prove that these many mysteries originated in mere clownish trickery, or perhaps an excessive taste for the cyclical.

"You can imagine, Olivier, how thoroughly I had forgotten all this. Nonetheless, when it came time to choose a topic for my degree in

Cendrier

Aesthetics, urged by my advisor to attempt some novel approach to the age-old question of pictorial esotericism, I found the memory of the bizarre Crucis opportunely flooding back into my mind. And so, leaving aside the familial anagrams, I resolved to devote my vacation to a brief inquiry. I supposed that a visit to the Bannière museum would bring me some insight, and I was not disappointed. A room on the upper floor revealed an unmistakable itinerary, through the order of the paintings' display. Like you, no doubt, I discovered—as was amiably confirmed by the museum's aged guide—that the central painting was an allegory, to be distinguished from the eight other works hanging around it. Now, setting off in a clockwise direction, starting from the allegory, my reading of those paintings' titles gave me this: *The Church of Bannière, The Square at Beaufort-le-Haut, The Park of Belarbre*— which is, I suppose, with its apocryphal crisscrossing flowers ornamenting the lawn, the canvas that your father saw painted —*The Outskirts of Cendrier, The Square at Chaumont, The Environs of Hautbois*, and *The Source of the Damier, Outside Monteaux.*

"Naturally it struck me that each of these proper names had a meaning, and that the paintings were hung in alphabetical order. My surprise, and yours too I suppose, if you attempted this experiment, reached its peak when, linking those towns in that order with lines on a map, I saw inscribed, despite the form's rela-

Cendrier

tive irregularity, the beginnings of a Maltese cross. Better yet, the three triangles of that incomplete figure were joined by their summits in the environs of Belcroix."

With a burst of laughter, Olivier interrupts her:

"Just as I said: in the area of Belcroix lies the center of the cross!"

"Does this not designate that city as the itinerary's endpoint? Why not go there, then, tell me?"

"Look, Atta."

No sooner is it presented between the traveler's fingers, beneath the clouded skies, than a glistening appears on the postcard below. The card takes the form of a colored rectangle, offering the details of a town square, viewed from above. At the center of the photograph, in the square's far left corner, a calvary erected on an octagonal plinth raises its cross high against the stormy sky. Such is the angle of the shot that the calvary seems, in a sense, to strike out the inscription behind it, formed of blue letters painted onto the ruddy wall enclosing a group of enormous constructions. It is nonetheless possible to read *Labora . . . re A. C.*, and hence to deduce that it is the syllable *toi* that the monument's shaft has obliterated.

To the left, beyond the leafless plane trees lining the avenue, we find the facade, medievally ornamented, of the Auberge du

Cendrier

Beau Manoir. On the far left, finally, stands an administrative building, distinguished as such by the flag diagonally overhanging the entrance. The presence of a uniformed officer and a tall black vehicle parked nearby might, if necessary, confirm that this is a police station.

The right-hand half of the photo is simpler. To the right of the calvary, a pile of dead leaves is burning, with all sorts of flourishes and meanders. Its base has already been reduced to ashes; from the summit, still smoldering, an undulating plume of smoke rises and blends with the thick overcast veiling the skies. On the far right, marking the square's center, stands an ornamental hillock, covered with minuscule bushes and topped by a fountain, whose spray is collected some way down the hill, then pours out afresh through all manner of basins and cascades.

The reverse side reveals this to be a genuine photograph of Belcroix's central square, viewed from a window of the asylum.

"I don't understand," Atta murmurs.

"And yet how clearly this photo displays every one of the elements composing Crucis's allegory! From left to right: the banner clutched by the soldier and the flag overhanging the policeman; the fortified château's walls and the medievally ornamented facade of the Auberge du Beau Manoir; the boughs of the oak and the leafless plane trees lining the avenue; the two calvaries; the area already destroyed by fire, with its ashes, its wisps of smoke,

Cendrier

its charred branches, and the base of the leaf pile, already reduced to ashes; the hillside suffering the ravages of a wildfire and the mound of leaves' smoldering summit, releasing an undulating plume of smoke; the few trees toward the top of the slope and the minuscule bushes ornamenting the square's artificial hillock; the short foaming line that describes a cascade's course through the trees and the fountain whose spray is collected some way down the hill, then pours out afresh. . ."

"All of which confirms Belcroix's central importance . . ."

"Or simply," Olivier interrupts, "that we are on the right trail. Believe me . . ."

As elsewhere in this province whenever a name holds some clear meaning, Cendrier—"Ashtray"—has ignited a quarrel between foes and champions of language-as-source. Touting the religious disputes of old and the smoldering conflicts they occasioned—among which, along with the auto-da-fés, the recurring reprisals, the surprise pillagings, we must no doubt include this very struggle between two opposed ideologies—some claim that the city's foundations were laid after a great fire had visited its desolations and ashes on the region's terrains. Pure conjecture, the others retort, undocumented in any written account: to posit the fiery destruction of putative chronicles as proof of such corroborative writings' existence is not only to fall back on a transparent ploy;

Cendrier

it is also, by insinuation, to lay the blame for those blazes at the feet of the opposite camp. Too, on the subject of those hypothetical pages, we must note the great difficulty, in any annalist's narrative, of distinguishing history from invention, so commonly are fanciful retrospections offered up as pure certainties.

On the other hand, there is no denying that Cendrier's name, as so often elsewhere, has brought to this spot many a deft artisan specialized in the confection of ashtrays. If various conflagrations have perhaps reduced more than one such studio to ashes, that is no unambiguous fact; for, in each case, the flames snuffed out a sign of language's guiding force only by simultaneously confirming it, through their own carbonizing action.

To be sure, the town's ashtray trade was encouraged by the nearby presence of a rich deposit of clay, unique in this calcareous region. If desired, everyday specimens of such wares may be procured from any local tobacconist; but the traveler is further urged to pay a call at the local museum of ceramics.

There every visitor might admire, judiciously divided among the eight rooms' display cases, a number of curious collector's items.

Playing on the idea that these receptacles' sole destiny is the containment of ashes, several artists, in times past, chose, by way of ornament and philosophy, to produce ashtrays resembling a vast

Cendrier

range of funerary urns. Others—enamellists specialized, let us note, in a particularly sumptuous shade of red—opted to portray, on the same theme, all manner of conflagrations. Of note is the disturbing and finely wrought series devoted to the province's various cities. Representing the village of Bannière, a broad oriflamme undulates silkily beneath the transparent glaze; in its center, the first flames of fast-spreading fire are nibbling away at the edges of the red Maltese cross. Superimposed on the brilliant red hues of a violent explosion, the mythical château of Beaufort strews its walls, towers, and crenellations over its environs. A third piece, designating Belarbre, silhouettes a venerable durmast against an opulent sunset, its dense greenery concealing all but the trunk, the main shaft, and two lateral branches, symmetrically placed. For Belcroix, they had only to subtract the tree's verdure and indent the outlines of the trunk and charred branches with the enveloping flames. As Cendrier's first houses appear at a bend in the road, Olivier remarks:

"I believe you may now make out the sense of the allegory as a whole?"

"I'm not entirely sure," Atta replies.

"From the soldier brandishing his banner on the left to the rounded hill with its cascades on the right, Crucis' vast canvas, no less than the various landscapes, depicts every stop on the road

Cendrier

to Monteaux. As for the ashtrays' innumerable scarlets, no doubt they evoke this region's conflicted and mysterious history."

Travelers drawn to the aged artifacts on offer in Beaufort-le-Haut will be amply rewarded by a stop at the La Cigale Bookstore, on the Rue des Octaves, specializing in regional folklore and arts.

"Unfortunately," says Atta, applying the brakes, "the building has all too clearly been destroyed. Someone has put up a notice—would you read it, Olivier?"

The young man approaches the paper affixed to the charred façade.

"What is it?" asks Atta.

"An invitation, in due form," Olivier replies. "Owing to the recent fire, M. Epsilon will until further notice receive visitors in his offices on the Place de l'Église, Chaumont."

Chaumont

"You had no difficulty discovering my whereabouts, then?"

"Why, of course not, Monsieur Epsilon," answers Atta, surprised. "The instructions could scarcely have been clearer."

"Could scarcely have been clearer, you say?"

"Indeed: 'Owing to the recent fire, M. Epsilon will until further notice receive visitors in his offices on the Place de l'Église, Chaumont.' "

"Ah yes, that, of course," says Epsilon, with a furtive glance at the young female idly scanning his books. "Still, there might well have transpired—how shall I say—some manner of incident. A child of the outskirts, finding himself with nothing to do, weary of the strange practices in which his peers sometimes indulge, might have set out to lacerate the card in a thousand ways, with all sorts of meanders and flourishes, do you see what I mean?"

"Not entirely, Monsieur, I admit . . ."

"Or perhaps simply the sun, or the rain, over time, might have washed out the writing, reducing it . . ."

"With all sorts of meanders and flourishes?"

". . . to a sort of misty landscape, a diffuse countryside, with its own strange geography, perhaps even its own curious folklore . . ."

Chaumont

"Pardon me for interrupting, Monsieur," Olivier says, "but before we arrive at the object of our visit, might I inquire if there is some familial relation between you and your homonym, the talented antiquarian of Beaufort-le-Haut?"

"Of course: he is in fact my brother. In that high place, he is maintaining an ancestral tradition."

"Would it be indiscreet to ask why you yourself do not persevere in your forefathers' footsteps?"

"The answer is quite simple—or, perhaps, on reflection, not so simple as it seems. Let us say that it stems from an intergenerational quarrel: my brother, as you might well imagine, is by some distance my elder. Now if, in times past, there was ever a certainty that seemed wholly beyond dispute, it was that things enjoyed an importance far superior to words. By one of those curious displacements into which perverse logics sometimes fall, that priority is further inscribed on the temporal axis, establishing an anteriority: all language is pre-existed, always, by some thing. Nonetheless, we may well wonder if one can truly conceive of a tree as such before one possesses its corresponding vocable."

"If I understand you correctly," says Olivier, "you are posing the crucial question that divides so many of this province's inhabitants?"

"And perhaps," Epsilon continues, "you will see a certain symbolism in the fact that two brothers should practice two such contrary fetishisms: things in his case, books in mine."

Chaumont

"This remark, dear Monsieur," says Olivier, "brings me to the purpose of our call.

"My friend and I are researching a painter who seems in his day to have exerted some influence in this region: Albert Crucis. You know of his work?"

"Certainly. What sort of research?"

"Scholarly," says Atta.

"Very good. Now, you know, every antiquarian harbors the naive hope that some exceptional, perhaps even mythical object —Golden Fleece, Grail, apples from the Garden of the Hesperides, who knows?—might one day, after countless peregrinations, fall into his hands. As for your labors, I believe I might prove helpful in more than one respect."

"Did the fire at La Cigale, in Cendrier, cause any irreparable losses?" Atta interrupts.

"Not at all. My most vital possessions I have always kept here, in secure storage."

"In sum," Olivier laughs, "there a *cigale*, here a *fourmi*."

"No doubt this allusion to La Fontaine is an opportune one, dear Monsieur, but I confess that it had occurred to me only partially: to my mind, the soprano cicada signified simply poetry. And also, for my insignia, a means of discreetly evoking the island of Malta, where, long ago, as a child, I delighted in solitary

Chaumont

strolls through the pines, amid the rustling of strident wings. But allow me to withdraw to my back room and retrieve something you may well be surprised to see in the hands of a book-lover as fervid as your humble servant."

At this hour of the day, nebulosity permitting, and providing the shop is suitably lit, the traveler will note that, from inside, the front window seems to offer a hybrid spectacle, superimposing the church's distant, shaded façade on the customers' reflected faces, closer by, amid the books, perhaps registering their sudden surprise at this sight.

"As you see," says Epsilon, returning, "I have here a canvas signed Albert Crucis. Note the characteristic minuscule cross taking the place of the dot on the *i*. No doubt playing on the ambiguity of the term, this work is entitled *Reflection*. Although there is no spiraling emblem on the window to tell us so, we find ourselves before an antiquarian's shop; rather than displaying his wares in a disorderly jumble, the merchant has assembled them into one unified scene, through which, on either side, in time, the outline of a whole story can be made out."

Affixed to the wall, facing the bed, a small engraving from the eighteenth century portrays a piquant scene. On the left-hand half of the paper, a profuse diversity of crosshatchings suggest, in both form and contour, the rumples, the creases, the cascades of

Chaumont

a canopy bed's sheets and curtains, at the far end of the room. Already close to the motionless turbulence of the linen and canvas, a man and a woman are half-struggling, entwined. Bent backward, the victim is endeavoring with her left hand to open the latch of the locked door, while her right, albeit with equivocal daintiness, pushes her assailant's torso away; meanwhile, the male is encircling her captive waist with his left arm, coolly closing the bolt with his right hand, and pressing his lips to the young woman's neck, causing her head to droop limply earthward, overcome with rapture. Four details—the well-tousled coiffure, a bared shoulder, the unbuttoned bodice, and the excessive dishevelment of the full skirt—render the scene entirely legible. After many ardent effusions of tenderness, betrayed by the bedclothes' disarray, the man, abruptly resolving to launch a decisive assault, has risen to check that the door is indeed locked. Seized by a sudden panic, his young friend, without troubling to straighten her clothing, has followed after, hoping to stop him . . . Along with a broad mirror, duplicating the ambiguous foes, a print of indecipherable design completes the chamber's decor.

Beyond the vast baldaquin bed, the attitude of the figures in an Aubusson-style tapestry is, in contrast, stamped with an almost ceremonious calm. In the background, an impeccable order rules the curtains and sheets of a canopy bed. Her posture erect, even somewhat stiff, eyes wide open, the lady stands facing the viewer,

Chaumont

her right arm hanging at her side, her left hand abandoned to her lover's caresses. Seen in one-quarter profile, the gentleman is reverently kissing the left breast offered up by the carefully unbuttoned bodice. The lady bears four rows of eight pearls in her severely coiffed hair. A shared kinship with purple unites the man's crimson garments with the blue of her dress, of the curtains, and of an indecipherable wall ornament.

In the shop itself, dressed in period costume, two mannequins match their poses and gestures to those of the decorative figures. In light of the bed's crimson silk curtains, there was no choice, if the tapestry was to be respected, but to reverse the clothing's hues. In a sumptuous, deep-cut crimson dress, the young lady sits on an invisible stool. Her black mane falls over her shoulders; her face is raised, eyes questioning, toward the man, who, towering over her, gazes self-assuredly down. Perhaps she has just given him leave to draw near enough to place one hand on her left shoulder, and the other in her hair. The entire scene is in any case easily imagined. Trusting, the girl has let herself be led into this room, but then, noting how closely the color of the bed's curtains matches her own dress, her cheeks have begun to burn.

The engraving, the tapestry, the bow and arrow affixed to the wall, the small heart-shaped table with a Dresden porcelain figurine of a gentleman kissing an elegant lady's hand, the strange figures or-

Chaumont

namenting the rug, every element of the room's decor has only added to her alarm. Approaching the blue-tinged, gilt-framed mirror, she discovers within it not the dimly imagined deliverance, but only those same troubling symbols, duplicated, and her own scarlet face. Her legs giving way, she collapses onto a stool, eyes fixed on the man as he slowly advances.

Seen from behind, a young couple stands holding hands on the sidewalk, peering into the window. Brunette, the woman wears a red dress; the man, blond, is clad in blue. Reflected head-on in the glass, their persons seem to insert two further figures into the shop's setting. But perhaps these two young people are simply admiring themselves, one beside the other, in that broad improvised mirror. Along with this pair, the shop window reflects the church's shaded facade, and, at the top, in what can be seen of the sky, a thick layering of white.

"Even with the signature and abundance of clouds, are you entirely certain of this work's authenticity?" says Olivier.

"I am indeed, Monsieur," answers Epsilon. "My brother assured me of that when he entrusted the canvas to me."

"But how can that be, since the painted display matches a show of antiques from an entirely posterior age . . ."

"Nothing could be simpler: it was from this very canvas that my brother drew the idea for that display."

"But all those objects," says Atta, "so similar . . ."

Chaumont

"Identical, you mean, Mademoiselle. They belonged to the painter, who naturally used them as his models. When his possessions were put up for sale—reasonably priced, as he wished—they were bought by my brother and his various colleagues, each according to his own speciality."

"All signs thus point," remarks Olivier, "to an insistent desire, on the painter's part, that such a display be mounted after his death. Aiming, I can only think, to lead the ill-informed observer, reversing the order of things, into viewing the display not as a result of the canvas, but rather, more naturally, as its model. Hence, postdated, the canvas proves to have been painted after the artist's death. We might no doubt suspect some secret intention in all this . . ."

"Speaking of which," says Atta, turning to Epsilon, "have you anything to tell us concerning his disappearance?"

"I suppose you are not unaware that, carried off one evening in an ambulance, he subsequently recovered his health, whereupon his friends conveyed him directly to a foreign country to further his convalescence. It was by way of a letter sent from a Baltic state, I believe, its blue stamp depicting a banner adorned with a horizontal lion, that his death was announced. In the course of a tour of that land's wooded mountains, the automobile transporting him had run off the road, at a bend revealed by a subsequent inquest to be both dangerous and seemingly needless; the car tum-

Chaumont

bled the length of the slope, finally coming to rest in a narrow stream, where its fuel ignited. After the explosion of the engine, the shattering of the chassis, and the mutilation of the corpse, the fire spread to the nearby trees, and on through the forest crowning the adjoining peak."

"Meaning," Atta remarks, "that no one can be sure he is genuinely dead!"

"Beware, Mademoiselle. Perhaps, in response to that anecdote, you are tempted today to evoke a myth apt to explain Crucis's tenacious prestige in these parts? Indeed, you might grasp the full extent of his influence if, as I recommend, you make for the Hôtel de La Fontaine, in Monteaux, and request the Display Room. There the traveler will find, reproduced with the aid of an ingenious transposition, the bedchamber of the present canvas.

"Too, you may find it worthwhile to read the mystical treatise titled *The Garden of Oppositions*, of which several exemplars may still be procured. Written by a former watchman of the park at Belarbre, under the unfortunate pseudonym *Asilus*, that work lays out, in the form of a journal, the experiments performed by a simple stroller over a period of eight months. Along with the author's abject eventual suicide by ingestion of a rare insecticide, we would do well to recall that book's dedication: *In homage to the living thought of my Master, A. C."*

Chaumont

"Crucis? Living thought?"

"Indeed, Mademoiselle, but I can offer you still other insights today, if you will consent to stray from the commonplace paths of reflection. Speaking of which, no doubt you have noted that the title of Crucis' painting, *Reflection*, apart from its psychological and optical senses, denotes a return. As for myself, you must understand that I sell books in my shop, perhaps, only in order to realize a metaphor."

"The bookdealer as allegory of the writer?" asks Lasius.

"Just so. But the principles governing my compositions are evidently not without eccentricity. Even full of finesse, of order, of charming surprises, of renewals, there is no attempt in my works to narrate a story. Rather, the aim is to derive a fiction from certain strict rules, established in the realm of abstractions. To that end, it was first necessary to find two antagonistic genres. Now, in their respective realizations, the guidebook and the novel stand starkly opposed: the one entirely effaces itself behind the world it invites its reader to see; the other, with its descriptions and adventures, always founds some new, unique universe in the weave of its language. It sufficed, then, to define the book as the site and the stakes of those two rivals' conflicts."

"Poetry versus realism, in short," Atta remarks. "Cicada versus ant . . ."

"If you like," Epsilon resumes. "Note, in any case, how unre-

lentingly the fiction is beset by those arbitrary alphabetical movements, even as that despotism is itself besieged by the enveloping unity of the events."

"Very well," says Olivier, "but how, in practice, to articulate
the two enemies' maneuvers? How to avoid the predictabilities of
so elementary a strategy?"

"Nothing could be simpler; for, with even the most minimal scrutiny, each adversary reveals within itself its own contestation.
There is no guide that does not succumb to the enticements of language, and that, along with its descriptions, presenting each object in some striking new light, does not itself offer a host of curious adventures, in the guise of legends or history. As for the novel,
however occupied it may be in inventing the autonomy of its own
space, it nevertheless does not fail to make constant use of the real
world's elements: a fictive landscape can establish itself only by
reference to everyday settings. Thus, far from offering an un-
equivocal sign, every sentence is most often shot through with un-
certainties. This interweaving rendered impossible the alternating use of blue and red ink, which, at the start, not without naivete,
I had assigned those two forces. Red letters would have had to be
placed in blue words, and blue letters in red."

"Granted," Olivier remarks, "though I don't entirely see how
this concerns our research."

"We're coming to that. While you are surely not unaware that

Chaumont

crucis is the Latin genitive of 'cross,' it may surprise you to learn that in various regions, and notably this one, the phrase 'Christ-cross row' is exactly synonymous with 'alphabet.' The traveler will thus note that the name 'Crucis' unites the problem's two aspects: the real world by the painter's person, language by the notion of the alphabet. Undeniably, then, Crucis must in the end play a central role in the battle's progression. Even at this very general level, we may glimpse an equivocal reversal of the sort that continually arises. Though the alphabet is the emblem of language, it designates too, as if in the second degree, the eminently alphabetical character of the guidebook, and thus, appropriately overturned, serves as the insignia of the real world's priority; though Crucis' literal person clearly belongs to the real world, his repeated insertion into the adventure compels him to obey the dictates of language, and so to pass, through these metamorphoses, into the camp of written fiction.

"The traveler will readily grant that so complex a struggle, involving the detail no less than the whole, can be realized only if the space of the conflict is formally defined from the start. By arbitrary decision, the book was divided into eight chapters, each with eight sections, equal in that their divergence from a basic size could not, on any pretext, exceed a chosen limit. From the broadest factors—geography, ideology, history . . .—to the merest minutiae, everything is ordered as a representation . . ."

"A metaphor?"

Chaumont

"... in a sense, of the initial antagonism. Geography: in order that the theory of language-as-creator might everywhere be opposed by the thesis of reality's primacy, it was essential that every locale be endowed with a meaningful name. Whence, not without an awkward and telling repetition of the syllable *bel*, the cities of Bannière, Beaufort, Belarbre, Belcroix, Cendrier, Chaumont, Hautbois, and Monteaux.

"Ideology: the populace is riven by the twin doctrines cleaving the book: the majority's common sense is on all sides opposed, with its own special force, by language's secretive sect. And of course every traveler will observe that those intertwined conflicts are, in myriad ways, founded in history. For here and there we still find, if only allusively, evocations of ancient ideological wars, piling one about-face, one tactical paradox on another. Thus, staunch believers in stone and soil might be found bewailing the fiery destruction of annals attesting, they claim, to previously existing châteaux. In this way, at the price of inflamed descriptions, they can insidiously accuse writing's devotees of various auto-da-fés."

"Indeed. I can now make out those conflicts, and those many threats on all sides," says Olivier, "but how can the novelistic armies hope to surmount the crucial advantage granted the guidebook by the sites' alphabetical ordering?"

Chaumont

"Simply by considering alphabetical order as an itinerary."

"But, geographically speaking, that leads to all sorts of unthinkable oddities, triangular circuits, intersecting trajectories."

"To be sure; and so the itinerary must be justified by some other means."

"Which is?"

"In the course of his visit, then, no traveler will have failed to see an equivalence between Crucis and the alphabet. To understand alphabetical order as a route to be followed is to submit one's travels to Crucis's dictates. I need hardly remind specialists like yourselves of the vast allegory, ringed by a series of eight landscapes, in a separate room on the top floor of the Bannière museum. Nor will it surprise you to learn that, by reciprocal confirmation, those landscapes and that allegory urge the viewer to embark on a tour defined by the ordering of the letters."

"If there is to be travel, there must be travelers."

"And so, in a major victory for the novel, there are two."

"Is that victory so certain? Might not a guidebook, to lay out a visit in less tedious form, suppose the presence of various fictive tourists, perhaps even grant them their own voices, their own mind, gestures, questions?"

"Certainly ... The battle is devious. The foe is often quick to parry the proof, to turn the ploy back on itself; at some stage of

Chaumont

the journey, prudence might incite him to support his antago-
nists' theses. Hence, some less debatable attacks may be in order.

"Those doctrinaires who see the world as obedient to language,
and even, in their extremism, force it into that mold through all
manner of subtle rethinkings, are no doubt only interpreting, in
the allegorical mode, the following process. An irrevocable decision decrees that the prose of each chapter be shaped by the name
constituting its emblem. Under the sign of Belarbre, for example,
a vast botanical network is abundantly visible, not only in the literal sense, but also in many a figurative turn of phrase. Further
trading the results of these curious proclivities back and forth between their respective domains, the eight names thus form the tri-
bunal by which language dictates its terms."

"Have you any palpable evidence of this?"

"See above. In the opening paragraph of Belarbre, the traveler
is invited to pass under a verdant arcade. In the second, as the text
flows on, he will see, by curious happenstance, a fragment of bark,
several leaves, some manner of twig. Unless he himself gathers
such objects from his surroundings and obediently casts them
into the prose at some point upstream. Further on, with a bit of attention, the visitor might also discover, among others, the metaphors 'several branches of the region's secret ramifying hydrogra-

Chaumont

phy.' Finally, should it be defined in that same domain, a traveler's first name, evoking a tree, will be Olivier."

"In short," says Olivier, "the absolute erudition that is yours could well guide us exhaustively through the entire book."

"Most assuredly."

"Such that, thanks to a universal distortion whose full extent is, I believe, now beginning to dawn on me, the whole of the guide-book's activity is irremediably enclosed within the novel."

"Just so."

"And thus we might well conclude that the doctrine whose roots you have herewith laid bare is simply an emanation of the novel itself, in its struggle to impose its own language and fiction on the guidebook, and on things."

"Perhaps."

"In that case, necessarily, you yourself, Monsieur Epsilon, here before us in your book-filled storeroom, can be nothing other than some textual invention . . ."

"Logically . . ."

"And we ourselves, logically, as you have speciously sought to insinuate, must be the two travelers, born of some legendary formal conflict. But, far from convinced by these outlandish claims, what has principally struck us is the fact that your entire story is constructed on information supplied from Beaufort by Monsieur 'L'Espion,' your brother, so well named by his anagram."

Hautbois

One day, without question, my theses, and the findings in which they are rooted, will lead one or two scholars to study my life down to its smallest details. Happily, my acts are of interest to no one today. Unnoticed, for instance, went the regular habit that long drew me out of my house in Hautbois every Sunday. Straddling my bicycle, I set off down the hill. Often, en route, though I find little charm in that city, I followed the short branch road to Belcroix, to call on a laboratory worker of my acquaintance. Finally I arrived in Belarbre and headed for Lenpois Park, which, as a title for the pages that follow, I have chosen to dub the Garden of Oppositions. An opportune circumstance later enabled me to take up lodgings not far from that spot, at the corner of an avenue whose name, recalling my habitual stop on those weekly excursions, urged me to cultivate the aforementioned friendship. Now a neighbor of the park, I was able to visit it every day, and so pursue my research in suitable depth. The present volume offers the fruits of that labor. Not in the form of a synthesis —which, in its strangeness, I am not sure I will ever see to com-

Hautbois

pletion—but rather as a journal, noting my thoughts' daily progress.

Written the evening of the events, these notes are untouched by any posterior deletion, save that I have struck out the dates, for no phenomenon recorded here in any way depends on the season or year. Throughout, then, I propose to write simply "today."

One further word. However entire my fervor, I have not lost my realism: the publication of this work will allow some to advance further down the path toward coherence, but from a predictable majority, I have no doubt, it will garner nothing but sarcasm, and occasional threats. Let me thus here anticipate those inevitable insinuations, and, mocking them, to adopt, as a pseudonym, this pejorative cluster of letters: Asilus.

Today, as I strolled down a side path in L. Park, a young lady caught my eye. It was her dress that first stopped me, for—red, flowing, elegant—it was made of a fabric quick to evoke, with her every slight movement, a tall, mobile flame. From behind, with all manner of subtle precautions, I drew nearer; meanwhile, she walked slowly onward, gesturing oddly.

Her gaze remained fixed on the ground, as if following, at the edge of the path, where the sand's irremediable disorder met the dense intricacies of the grass, the shadows of her hands, now together, now suddenly apart.

Hautbois

Sometimes, after a quick glance around her, she bent down and carefully studied the ground.

Then she stood upright, resuming her operations a bit further along.

A smile on my lips, I briefly imagined approaching this young person, and, before she had raised her eyes, asking:

"Is it for my benefit that you make those strange signals?"

"No, of course not," she would perhaps have replied, with a start.

And then I:

"That's a pity; I like nothing more than deciphering signs."

But I hesitated. Such an opening line, in its banality, must already have been handed her many a time. Indeed, I thought, it might almost have come from some classic repertoire, with a natural rejoinder:

"Sorry to disappoint you, but I was simply, as I strolled these magnificent pathways, casting various shadow forms on the ground, my thoughts elsewhere."

"And what is your repertoire?"

Thus, by a curious mirror effect, my definition of the scene would have intervened in my discourse itself, and no doubt the girl would have answered:

"A cat, a goat, a dog, a swan . . ."

Hautbois

"Would you show me? Oh! Very good; do you know many others?"

"No. Only an elephant, a rabbit, a fly, a fish. You know," she would have added with a laugh, "I'm no expert in ombromania . . . And you?"

This response left me shaken. Forbidding any further retort in my mute dialogue, such as the question, not unbantering, of whether that was an ailment as serious as pyromania, the girl had gone on her way without looking back.

Glancing down as I passed toward the site of her operations, and noting a lively swarm on the sunlit sand at the edge of the lawn, I followed the young female until her red silhouette disappeared, among the visitors' green dresses and brown suits, into a more frequented area.

A thick layer of white veiled the sun as I retraced my steps. On the ground, at a spot easily located thanks to the bed of oblique flowers on the adjoining lawn, the few scattered ants displayed no notable agitation.

Today. Not by chance, this time, did I find myself heading for Belarbre and its park, but rather in response to an attraction so powerful that it surprised even me.

"Listen, Olivier. Before reading further into this little tome, I believe we must dare to divulge certain secrets of a more profound nature."

Hautbois

"Oh?"

"All signs suggest that you know I have already read the preceding text. I discovered it in my university's library. Almost of its own accord, the dictionary of contemporary painters, published in 1908, fell open to Albert Crucis' entry, revealing these two folded sheets, their edges ravaged by various rips and tears. No doubt they had once served as a bookmark. That was why, in my surprise, when you approached in the park and inquired if it was for your benefit that I made those strange signals, the reply 'no, of course not' sprang quite naturally to my lips. To hear you respond that this was a pity, as you liked nothing more than deciphering signs, only added to my alarm. Nevertheless, collecting myself, I was able to pursue the game of our dialogue . . ."

"That elaborate assemblage of passwords . . ."

"How so?"

"Is a specialist not always an initiate into some form of esotericism? Noting your silken red dress and odd gestures, I believed such an opening might serve as a sign of my recognition."

"You were not wrong, Olivier, and that was precisely the source, at the start, of my terror. Given all the violence and mysteries already amassed around Albert Crucis's figure, think of your knowledge's effect on my mind. But what troubles me now is my certainty, almost entire, that our acts were controlled by the

Hautbois

unthinkable rule that the book-dealer revealed. In the course of
our meeting, did our behavior not, by definition, conform to the
letter of this little text? Is there no . . . ?"

"That you were shaken by that book-crazed old Maltese ma-
niac I will gladly believe, but I cannot accept that his claptrap
overcame your convictions. Did you not see the disapproval, the
surprise, the panic inscribed on his face when, through a series
of questions in the preceding chapter, I forced him to admit that
his enterprise presupposed both him and ourselves to be mere
novelistic inventions, issued from some formal conflict?"

"I certainly do not claim, Olivier, that we are only figures in
some book. Everything disputes that absurdity: above us, the sky,
with its thick layers of white; all around us, the greenery, endlessly mobile, diverse, intricate; and the insects today, innumerable, active, scurrying over the grass; and you; and me; and us . . .
What book could contain all that? But suppose, on the other hand,
that, unbeknownst to us, every one of our deeds, like our encounter in the park, obeys the specific directives of a text buried
in some distant library . . ."

"Nonsense. The act we were playing when we first met was entirely conscious."

"Perhaps, as Crucis might say, that scene was simply a metaphor for workings of some deeper kind."

Hautbois

"If you believe Asilus's work has such power, Atta, let us return to our reading, since I too found only the first tattered pages in the 1908 dictionary . . ."

Today. Not by chance, this time, did I find myself heading for Belarbre and its park, but rather in response to an attraction so powerful that it surprised even me. Very slight was my disappointment at the girl in red's absence; I could thus only conclude, as I strolled through the gardens, that my true curiosity lay elsewhere. An extraordinary agitation could be seen on the sand at my feet. Everywhere the ants were battling, in miniature skirmishes: the weaker blue race, currently vanishing, and the red, triumphant, gigantic. My scrutiny succeeded in isolating a melee pitting a giant red specimen against a squad of minuscule blue soldiers. Although fighting unaided, its superior size and vigor offered the greater ant victory time after time. Around it lay several tiny assailants, already maimed. Despite the occasional influx of reinforcements, I little doubted this brawl's outcome; but then I perceived, amid that mobile confusion, the contours of an underlying order. At that moment a cloud veiled the sun. The soldiers broke off their engagement and scattered; soon no trace of these struggles remained to be seen on the ground.

Today, after several weeks' hiatus occasioned by the recent bad weather, the birth of my son, and the death of his mother, I re-

Hautbois

turned to the park under a pure azure sky. I succeeded in isolating, in the midst of the broader battle, one easily observed clash, and the order that appeared to govern it. Though often diverging to rescue some comrade in danger, the assailants were gradually driving the fight toward the shadow cast on the ground by several blades of grass, imperceptibly trembling. And then, all at once, an astounding development: no sooner had the giant insect entered the shade, in pursuit of its prey, than the battle's character was reversed. Along with these curious turnabouts, the traveler will note the delicacy of the shadows inscribed on the sands' minute disorder by the neighboring lawn. Suddenly the huge fighter's movements were marked by an unexpected torpor. And since, contrarily, its tiny opponents seemed invested with a new vitality, the beast was promptly brought to its knees, and severed into its constituent parts.

Today. After much meditation, much reading, and a talk with my friend in Belcroix, I have come to accept that my study commands me to take sides. Arriving on site, I raised my hand to inscribe a shadow onto the field of combat. Instantaneously, with an abrupt massacre of the large creatures, the battle's lineaments were transformed.

Today. With a rapidity that astounds me, the ants of both camps have adapted to my interventions, shifting their tactics accordingly. No sooner did my hand's shadow land on the ground than—

Hautbois

even before any fighting broke out—the red ants fled the sector at once, while the others, contrarily, rushed in.

Today. I had the idea of gathering every possible tiny assailant within my hand's shadow, then slowly leading them into the sunny patch held by their foes. Several red ants were caught unawares by the raiders' audacity.

Today. Their response, in its excellence, did not fail to surprise me. Four mighty warriors hurried to encircle the moving shadow; if I suddenly moved my hand toward one of these, several of my protégés were exposed, unavoidably, on the darkened zone's opposite side. They were immediately assaulted and felled.

And if, hoping to come to their aid, I drew my hand backwards, it was now the first group of ants that lost their support. Then I attempted a series of lively, disordered motions over the battlefield. A catastrophe! In the panic ensuing from these haphazard effects, the natural might of the red ants prevailed. The commando squad's volunteers were methodically slaughtered as I looked on.

Today. A terrible night, riddled with nightmares. The insects' antagonisms have begun to reverberate onto new planes, metamorphosing into all manner of human conflicts. Now it was a crusade; turning around, I glimpsed, on a town square, the recruitment of the volunteers. The sun had emerged from the clouds. Eight strangers stood at one corner of the square, shaking the dust

Hautbois

from their tunics. One raised a banner embroidered with the emblematic cross, then planted its shaft in the gap separating four cobblestones. These instigators of the Crusade had come to awaken ardors and strike fear into the soul. Perhaps their orator spun out rousing descriptions contrasting the inferno's red flames with the delicate azures of paradise. No doubt he evoked the primordial rivalry of goods and evils, and how this subterranean struggle sometimes surfaces in the form of fierce battles, each one apparently decisive, in the heat of which any attempt at indifference equates to support for the opposite side.

The lavish phantasmagoria inscribed in every mind by these words left the audience shaken. Instantly the adolescents' passions were inflamed. Their elders—fathers or brothers—discreetly endeavored to distract them from the flag's snapping billows, amid which the cross, continually metamorphosing, seemed alternately to vanish and to be reborn. In vain: some had been contaminated, and already these efforts to curb the mounting inspirations swelling their breasts struck them as sacrilege. Several ran off at a breakneck pace, eager to snatch up some garment and appear at the imminent departure; a number of others, their imaginations not nimble enough to call up the splendid Orient, were convinced indirectly, by the determination of family or friends.

Now it was an engraving. On the left-hand half of the paper, a profuse diversity of crosshatchings suggested, in both form and

Hautbois

contour, the rumples, the creases, the cascades of a canopy bed's sheets and curtains, at the far end of the room. Already close to the motionless turbulence of the linen and canvas, a man and a woman were half-struggling, entwined. Bent backward, the victim was endeavoring with her left hand to open the latch of the locked door, while her right, albeit with equivocal daintiness, pushed her assailant's torso away; meanwhile, the male was encircling her captive waist with his left arm, coolly closing the bolt with his right hand, and pressing his lips to the young woman's neck, now it was a learned debate, full of wily ripostes. Even full of finesse, of order, of charming surprises, of renewals, there is no attempt here to narrate a story. Rather, the aim is to derive a fiction from certain strict rules, established in the realm of abstractions. To that end, it was first necessary to find two antagonistic genres. Now, in their respective realizations, the guidebook and the novel stand starkly opposed: the one entirely effaces itself behind the world it invites its reader to see; the other, with its descriptions and adventures, always founds some new, unique universe in the weave of its language. It sufficed, then, to define the book as the site and the stakes, now their response, in its excellence, did not fail to surprise me. Four mighty warriors hurried to encircle the moving shadow; if I suddenly moved my hand toward one of these, several of my protégés were exposed, unavoidably,

Hautbois

on the darkened zone's opposite side. They were immediately assaulted and felled. And if, hoping to come to their aid, I drew my hand backwards, it was now the first group of ants that lost their support. Then I attempted a series of lively, disordered motions over the battlefield, and I woke up today.

I can pursue my endeavors no further without devising some plausible justification for my odd gestures over the sand. When confronted by persistent stares or casual queries, I will, hewing to a well-known dialogue, reply

that I was simply, as I strolled these magnificent pathways, casting various shadow forms on the ground, my thoughts elsewhere. In response to the question "and what is your repertoire?" I will have no great difficulty citing the names of various animals.

Today. As a precaution, I trained myself, on neutral ground, to orient my hands in such a way as to obtain the shadows of a cat, a goat, a dog, a swan, and then, preparing for every possible threat, those of an elephant, a rabbit, a fly, a fish.

Today. I made use of a high plane-tree branch, with its many leaves and its twigs. Sheltered by this complex, slow-moving shadow, a multitudinous squadron advanced. It soon triumphed handily over its unsuspecting foes.

Today. A fire broke out in my garden. The weather was scorch-

Hautbois

ing hot, and the sun's rays, concentrated and cast onto several dried blades of grass by a fragment of broken bottle, produced the initial flame. I was able to extinguish it immediately.

Today. Never before had I spotted that small shard of glass; otherwise, I would certainly have removed it at once.

Today. As for the dried grasses, it cannot be denied that their careful arrangement, radiating from the central focal point, assigned eight divergent trajectories to the nascent flames.

Today. The enemies have found a response to the tactic of the shaken branch. I panicked. In their disorder, my agitations once again produced a disastrous result.

Today. Strategic considerations of a most singular sort flood my mind. Often, their strange subtleties compel me to drive them away.

Today. They have come back.

Today. So obsessed am I with my research that the world of ants has come to seem, curiously, far more vital than that of men.

Today. They have come back.

Today. I have learned from a book that certain fires ravaging the island of Malta are thought to have been set by ants. It would seem that a skillful arrangement of glass shards in the bright sunlight allows these creatures to lay waste to their enemies' colonies.

Today. Obeying, in its every detail, an imperious impulse, I have perfected a new mode of intervention: a small stack of cards,

Hautbois

with a series of ever-smaller ellipses cut from their centers. Scanning the area in dispute, I quickly distinguished a massive red fighter. At the price of many a frantic maneuver, I enclosed the creature within the sunlit ellipse outlined by the first card. Protected by the shade, several of my allies huddled along the curved border surrounding the prisoner. The deployment of a second card, then a third, reduced the illuminated area. A fourth changed the ellipse's orientation, and the ant immediately adjusted its position. It stood perfectly still. Its antennae alone, at the top of its head, remained vigorously active. The spectacle gives rise to a curious emotion, distant, as if ancestral, and demanding intervention. With many a fit and start, the following cards gradually shrank the sunlit zone until it virtually matched the encircled creature's dimensions. Rather than assailing the prisoner from all sides, my friends were content merely to draw ever nearer. From the last card was cut a long, vacant corridor, offering a means of escape. The prisoner hurtled into it

blindly. Gaining the open sand, it began running in all directions, attacking, felling, slaughtering its own comrades. Soon it was corralled by a crowd of its fellows. A few moments later, the lunatic lay severed into its constituent parts.

Today. Preparing to cross the Avenue de Belcroix, I was nearly run down by a red automobile, driven at breakneck speed.

Hautbois

Today. It is not without some surprise that I consider the impulse that led me to note the automobile incident in this journal of my labors.

Today. In my garden, I saw the rays of the setting sun gathered into the minuscule gleam of a fragment of bottle glass, which I did not fail to remove at once.

Today. No longer can I hold back the hypotheses little by little kindled within me by the imperious dreams of a memorable night. There can no doubt that all human history, with its quests for love, wealth, fleeting liberty, or the hollow emerald of the Grail, with its wars, its aesthetics, its revolutions, its crusades, merely replicates the pitiless battles waged, over many millennia, by the ant populations. Should he ponder the nature of this correspondence, the traveler will at first not fail to be troubled by the simple idea that human activities might be a metaphor for the conflicts dividing the microscopic folk. I am led to believe, however, that the link is far more specific than that. Who, after countless hours of detailed study, will one day devote a thesis to the vital role played by stowaway ants, transported by ship from one end of the world to the other at the time of the Crusades? Who will explain, via these insects and their influence, the surprising triumphs and expansions of many peoples versed in enigmatic cults, or involuntarily producing delectable foodstuffs? Who will set out to define all revolutions, wars, and aesthetics as mere impulses wholly gov-

Hautbois

erned by the miniature tribes? And indeed, who will doubt that the culprit who loosed his automobile on my person, or strewed my garden with fragments of glass, leaving to the red insects the simple task of adjusting the shards' position and arranging the flammable grass, was merely obeying certain suggestions sent from high places? Who will refuse to accept how unrelentingly today I am spied on, cursed, and threatened?

Today. At long last I am able to bring into play the specific insecticide whose concept recently sprang to my mind. Should its use be allowed to spread, the result will no doubt be tremendous ...

I am deeply apprehensive of the publication of this little tract, but I do not suppose that avoidance of risk can forestall the workings dominating me on all sides. And furthermore, what are the perils menacing me next to those that await the agents who will one day no doubt come, on various secret missions, sent by the enemy powers? It is in any case with the certainty of my inspiration's extraordinary origin, and with pride in my role as accessory to a lofty plan, that I here put an end to this line, today.

"I don't understand," says Atta. "Really, I cannot imagine why the book-dealer Epsilon recommended this claptrap. Contending as it does that all human thoughts and deeds are inspired by the imperceptible peoples, is this unthinkable mystic's dogma not irre-

Hautbois

ducibly opposed to the no less absurd idea that all things stem from language and formal conflicts?"

"No doubt," answers Lasius. "But surely, even as you define that contradiction, you can surmise Epsilon's likely rejoinder. Since the novel has inverted the principle of the guidebook so utterly as to make it, tendentially, a pilot of the text, *The Garden of Oppositions* offers itself as a counterattack. Rather than allowing things written to come into being, does not the journal format deployed by this text assign language the subordinate function of noting only that which has already occurred? And with this, the attentive traveler will note the devious ploy by which, through an immoderate use of the word 'today,' *The Garden of Oppositions* seeks to retrospectively annex the preceding pages, previously strewn, for that very purpose, with many gratuitous uses of that selfsame adverb.

"To this, I am sure, it might be replied that those lines of red and blue ants, their legs protruding on either side of the words' axis, were, to cite Crucis's phrase, only a metaphor for the text, since it was in such alternating colors that the author first planned to lay down his prose. To obey the ants' directives, then, is, in the final analysis, to draw one's inspiration from the text itself.

"But let us not lose ourselves in Epsilon's bizarre theories, nor allow them to divert us from the road to ..."

"Monteaux?"

Monteaux

"Wait. That would be premature."

"But the Hôtel de La Fontaine, dear Olivier, with its Display Room, so mysterious, so allusive, so full of promise . . ."

"To be sure, Atta, I do not doubt we are nearing the denouement; and, for that very reason, before we continue our journey, a brief recapitulative tableau seems in order. From the intersection, near Belcroix, of the lines linking several of our itinerary's stops on the map, you had deduced that this city, which I preferred to avoid, had some central importance. This was in fact, to your mind, confirmed beyond doubt by the photograph snapped from the asylum, and its concordance with Crucis's allegory. I must grant that your judgment was sound. Indeed, its strange manifest content aside, Epsilon's conversation teems with useful clarifications. Asserting that, by arbitrary decision, the book was divided into eight chapters, each with eight sections, equal in that their divergence from a basic size could not, on any pretext, exceed a chosen limit, he instilled in us, for example, voluntarily or no, the idea of a grid formed of eight squares by eight. With that figure inscribed in our minds, the subsequent enumeration of the eight

Monteaux

cities inclined us, first of all, to realize that every name was composed of eight letters, and then, immediately and consequently, to place those letters into the grid thus supplied, whereupon it becomes abundantly clear that the square's diagonal sends the sonorities of 'Belcroix' cascading down its slope. In other words, we might say that this city is designated by the flowing, oblique alignment of the first letter of the first name, the second of the second, and so on, until the last of the last. Here, look."

Olivier inspects the disorderly cache beneath the windshield. Thus, in succession, his left hand encounters a glove, the handle of the magnifying glass today, the comb, the red, white-lined handkerchief, and the leaflet, in whose margin he writes, each time displacing the capital by one step, the province's various names: Bannière, bEaufort, beLarbre, belCroix, cendRier, chaumOnt, hautboIs, monteauX.

"In sum," Atta remarks, "you are showing the utility of a slanted reading."

"Yes, but only after the text has been recognized, previously and indubitably, within its formal grid."

"And how to interpret the X that marks the series' conclusion? A cross?"

"Or perhaps an unknown quantity . . ."

"Furthermore," Olivier resumes, "this hypothesis has the advantage of conferring some meaning on the anomalies of the vast Cru-

Monteaux

cis canvas displayed at Bannière. You are not unaware that, rising diagonally, the smoke pales, metamorphoses toward the left, and finally melds with the ponderous white tones of a thundercloud lurking in the skies, nor that, in this way, the wind that propels them controverts, on the other end of the canvas, the moderate breeze rippling the flag rightward. You know, too, that the soldier on the left is gazing rightward, whereas the water, its source on the right, flows leftward until, now stilled, it mirrors the calvary's cross. Each of these antagonisms can be read as a convergence, designating Belcroix. Better yet: if we turn today to the photograph snapped from the asylum, we will note, on the left, in the square's furthest corner, a calvary erected on an octagonal plinth. Such is the angle of the shot that the calvary seems, in a sense, to strike out the inscription behind it, formed of blue letters painted onto the ruddy wall enclosing a group of enormous constructions. It is nonetheless possible to read *Labora . . . re A. C.*, and hence to deduce that it is the syllable *toi* that the monument's shaft has obliterated. Now, a cross can be used both to indicate and to annul. In this case, I believe the former reading is the one to be favored.

"Should you require some further proof that we might usefully pay a call at the laboratory, I would draw your attention to the leaflet in whose margins I have just written: an instruction manual, as it happens, for the colorant known as fluorescein, which you no doubt thought of using, if necessary, to discover various enigmatic fluid networks beneath the landscapes' surface. And this

Monteaux

benzene derivative is produced, says the parenthesis inscribed after the title, 'by the Laboratoire A.C., Belcroix.'"

"What I find most surprising, dear Olivier, is your longstanding wish to defer a journey toward a locale betrayed by such a profusion of signs."

"There is no mystery to my motive. I have unerringly followed the letter of Crucis's prescription, which insisted that each town be traversed one single time. Nonetheless, my perplexity mounted as all manner of details, endlessly multiplied, designated Belcroix as an essential stop. On first nearing that city, after Belarbre, my knowledge was as yet insufficient to make the visit a fruitful one. It was then I remembered a legend that, in his unthinkable book, Asilus links to the conflicts of the tiny tribes. One day, writes Chrétien de Troyes, Percival witnesses the rites of an enigmatic cult, but, in his naiveté, fails to realize that this ceremony concerns the very object of his quest; only later, after long learning in his various adventures, will he attain the Grail, its emerald cup and its precious liquid. Knowing, then, that the visit would be premature, I was able to say, with no great untruth, that Belcroix had offered me its secrets already, and that I had no intention of wandering, without motivation, at the mercy of every spectacle, random and minuscule, that might hold me back."

"Truth to tell, Monsieur Lasius . . . incidentally, if I may inquire in passing, has anyone ever told you of the creatures whose name you bear?"

Monteaux

"No, no one."

"It is true that *Lasius alienus* are words apt to be found solely in specialized works, in the course of the most arduous studies. Such is the name of a race of tiny dark ants . . . But to answer your question, Monsieur: the events you speak of date some sixteen years back, which is to say eight years before Monsieur Gallois' death in an unthinkable accident. It was one of those superb autumn days, when, above the reddening boughs, the blue of the sky is assailed only by ponderous layerings of white. As my employee was leaving the building, a plummeting roof-tile struck him square on the skull. So intense was the emotion among the scene's witnesses that one onlooker, I will never forget it, began to admire aloud the beauteous harmony of the red terra-cotta and the bloodstain inscribed thereupon. Might I confess? It was less the untimeliness of his assessment that shocked me than its diametrical contrast to my own. Rather, the true splendor was today to be found in the abundantly flowing crimson, veering toward violet, against the victim's blue shirt! All of which suggests, if I may note this in passing, that, by undoing our everyday certainties, an accident liberates within us not only dismay, but also a more percipient gaze . . . This was, for my business, an irreparable loss: no matter the circumstance, I never failed to seek Monsieur Gallois' counsel. It was he, for example, who advised me on the color of our walls and our sign. And while at first that curious alliance—or rather that conflict—between blue and red had greatly sur-

Monteaux

prised me, I must admit that in time it came to seem the obvious choice. Meticulous, hardworking in the extreme, he had insisted on determining the letters' exact placement himself, and since, alas, the presence of his son, a dangerous pyromaniac, offered him access to the asylum across the square, he did not hesitate to appraise the general effect, as the work progressed, from a window on the fourth floor. The fine photo he took of our grounds was in fact later used by a printer of postcards. An exemplar of that precious document may be readily obtained today from any bookdealer or souvenir shop in the region. To be sure—but this trait has always struck me as a sure mark of genius—Gallois' doings were, as a whole, not without oddity. He enjoyed reading tortuous doctrines in singular books, and often devoted himself to studies whose utility seemed of the most dubious sort.

"Thus it was that, at the instigation of his friend, the park watchman of whom you speak, who made his name known through a deranged little tome titled *The Garden of Oppositions*, he threw himself zealously into the search for a special insecticide capable of slaying one single race of ants. Despite the disruptions visited on his work by recurring bouts of a Maltese fever, he soon discovered that absurd poison in the form of a crimson liquid that would eventually permit, in the most pathetic of circumstances, the death of the one who had ordered it."

Monteaux

"Is the formula of this unlikely product known?" asks Olivier.

"No, Monsieur. Shortly before Gallois' death, a terrible fire consumed his home from basement to attic, with all sorts of meanders and flourishes. A most lamentable matter: the fire had been started by Gallois' own son, released from the asylum only eight days before, having been judged harmless. Tearfully, he acknowledged his guilt, protesting that he had once again found himself unable to resist certain strange impulses beyond his control. Could there be a truer definition of the alienated mind? Thus, one single event cost Gallois both his home and his son. For all his force of character, and despite his profound intelligence, a mental disturbance seized him for a period of several hours, and with it the conviction that these happenings were rooted in some obscure act of vengeance . . ."

Olivier interrupts:

"Might there still exist a sample of this bizarre elixir?"

"Yes, Monsieur, one single specimen, stowed today in the laboratory, in a drawer marked with an X."

"May we see it?" asks Atta.

"Certainly, Mademoiselle. In the meantime, allow me to offer you a cigarette. One of these, for example, eminently suited to the occasion, less for the two opposed creatures inscribed against a red field than for the slogan 'Wherever particular people congregate,' which we might in our own idiom construe as 'Wherever sin-

Monteaux

gular people come together.' Excuse me; I must leave you for a few moments . . ."

"Listen, Olivier darling, I wonder if this gentleman's ramblings, in their sterile abundance, may not be distracting us from investigations of a more profound nature. Rather than this mediocre office today, I picture us in Monteaux, at long last, in the Display Room. In their form and contour, the rumples, the creases, the cascades of a canopy bed's sheets and curtains can be seen at the far end of the room. Already close to the motionless turbulence of the linen and canvas, the two of us are half-struggling, entwined. Bent backward, I endeavor with my left hand to open the latch of the locked door, while my right, albeit with equivocal daintiness, pushes your torso away; meanwhile, you encircle my captive waist with your left arm, coolly closing the bolt with your right hand, and pressing your lips to my neck, causing my head to droop limply earthward, overcome with rapture. Four details —the well-tousled coiffure, a bared shoulder, the unbuttoned bodice, and the excessive dishevelment of the full skirt—render the scene entirely legible. After many ardent effusions of tenderness, betrayed by the bedclothes' disarray, you, abruptly resolving to launch a decisive assault, have risen to check that the door is indeed locked. Seized by a sudden panic, I, without troubling to straighten my clothing, have followed after, hoping to stop you . . ."

Monteaux

"Here is the object in question," the director announces, entering.

"As you may see for yourselves, I have here a vial of somewhat unusual color, rather akin to an emerald. Before moving on from this laboratory, might a certain traveler desire a few final details concerning that tint's motivation? If memory serves, exposure to light, over time, threatened the precious fluid with an insidious adulteration. Comfortable only in darkness, it had, for its preservation's sake, to be housed in some sheltered compartment, guarded by a protective crystal. Superimposed, the translucent emerald and crimson give the liquid an appearance identical to black ink. For this reason, its inventor, perhaps as a small pleasantry, perhaps out of prudence, liked to refer to this flask as his 'inkwell.' But I do not think he might have pursued that allegory so far as to dip some plume into the fluid, with the aim of composing a book . . ."

"Would you be so kind," says Atta, "as to show me that equivocal object?"

With a wealth of precautions, the director now proffers the crystal. But, the traveler will note, so profound is Atta's emotion that her hands tremble, shake, and suddenly let the offering drop to the floor.

"Oh, dear!"

Monteaux

A minuscule cataclysm ensues, with the precious fluid's last drops pouring from the broken glass. In her dismay, perhaps, Atta has raised her hands to her crimson cheeks. Mounting inspirations swell her breast.

"I'm so sorry . . ."

But already a torrent of comforting words is directed her way. The industrialist assures her that the vial's value was purely symbolic; falling back on a commonplace, he adds, not unceremoniously:

"Besides, to lose one secret is to recapture eight more!"

Then, as Olivier begs his pardon for their visit and the girl's inexcusable clumsiness, he escorts them, with a thousand cordialities, to his establishment's door.

"I little thought," Olivier remarks, "that such an object might so violently perturb your behavior."

The young female smiles. Soon a laugh, unrestrained, parts her lips.

"Don't play the innocent, darling. I need hardly inform you, of all people, that with a painter as meticulous as this, nothing must be neglected. You will recall that, in the old gentleman's absence, I allowed myself to evoke, in parodic counterpart to a discourse spun out by the book-dealer Epsilon, what might soon transpire between us in the Display Room. Now, just when the exercise of that description was beginning, profoundly, to excite even me, the old madman entered, announcing and brandishing his find, such

Monteaux

that my mind could not help but glimpse in that object, instantly, a masculine symbol. Think of my emotion when, a moment later, the vial was placed in my hands."

"But had you not asked for it?"

"No doubt, but, in order to convey my state of mind, must I really, surmounting my modesty, dare to divulge certain secrets of a more profound nature? And in any case, is the loss of that dusty glasswork in that mediocre place really so serious?"

"Certainly not, Atta. Think no more of it. And since, as per Crucis's wish, such is our itinerary's last stop, drive us now, without further delay, to Monteaux."

"How far might that be in kilometers, incidentally?"

"Around one hundred twenty, I think."

"There's no one to run over this time, though . . ."

The young man laughs. By various maneuvers, he seeks a more comfortable position. Finally he lifts his right arm and places it, cautiously, on his neighbor's seat back. The visitor will note that his hand immediately encounters a lock of black hair, minimally mobile. Idly closing together, the index and middle finger imprison the dark tress. Soon, with minuscule motions, the other fingers join in, then move on to the right shoulder, and there engage in diverse limited wanderings. Whereupon, in a grave voice, the young man declares:

"I may now inform you that the notes preserved in my father's

117

Monteaux

suitcase include a certain strange text in which, oddly, Crucis's influence coincides with the bookdealer's absurd thesis. For everything, in that autobiographical fragment, depends on the alphabet. The text's licentious nature, as you will soon understand, long compelled me to defer its description. There Christophe Lasius describes the excellent amorous results he derived from the use, not of some mysterious philtre today, but of a precious list of itineraries. Limiting to eight the number of spots where his skills could be exercised with suitable virtuosity, he consulted various dictionaries to find their equivalents in seven other languages. These lists he then ordered alphabetically, dubbing them 'nations,' on the example of the Order of Malta. Each nation thus charted a precious storyline: in English, for instance—belly, breasts, mouth, nape, neck, pubis, shoulders, thighs—or in French— mouth (*bouche*), neck (*cou*), thighs (*cuisses*), shoulders (*épaules*), nape (*nuque*), pubis (*pubis*), breasts (*seins*), belly (*ventre*), etc. In a brief commentary on this procedure, he attributes its potency to its rigorously arbitrary nature, and to the host of surprises thereby allowed.

"Naturally, he did not wish to limit himself to such short-lived narratives. Drawing up each list in each of the chosen languages, he obtained eight possible roadmaps for far longer sagas. The English version, for instance, making use of the English, Finnish, French, German, Latin, Polish, Spanish, and Swedish lists; or the

Monteaux

French, which assembled the German (*allemand*), English (*anglais*), Spanish *(espagnol)*, Finnish (*finlandais*), French (*français*), Latin (*latin*), Polish (*polonais*), and Swedish (*suédois*). Repetitions included, each tale is thus composed of sixty-four parts. Between these two extremes, of course, the system leaves room for intermediary combinations: in no way did the author forbid himself the possibility of following several routes simultaneously over a given body. For coherence's sake, I should add that it was in one of the more complete ceremonies, says the manuscript, that my person was conceived. But keep on straight ahead, if you please, toward the hilltop."

"But what about the village? The Hôtel de La Fontaine? The room?"

"Don't worry, darling. Monteaux is the *mont des eaux*—the hill of the waters. There, beneath a profusion of wild greenery, lies the Damier's source. Thus, our entire story, starting from Bannière, is perhaps, in a sense, a return to the origin. There, take that turn to the left . . ."

"But it's nothing more than a dirt road, invaded on all sides by the brush."

"In situations of burning urgency, must we recoil before certain sacrifices?"

"Darling, your determination is beginning to frighten me a little."

Monteaux

"Let us continue on foot toward that impossible place—over there, betrayed by the sunlight's more unbroken glow through the trees . . . Very good. Among the locals, this clearing is known by the name *Les Essarts*."

"Meaning?"

"In a general sense, an *essart* is any wooded tract burned off for agricultural use. I suppose that the farmers of this calcareous region were hoping here to begin one of their typical checkerboard squares: the source of the Damier is not far away. In spite of the rustling branches, you can hear its cascade, further down. They must have abandoned their work, as the clearing's dimensions are modest, and already various bushes have grown back. Now undress."

"But darling, you must be mad. Here? Now? Just like that?"

"Just like that. Do you find the surroundings insufficiently wild? First the belt encircling your waist. Now, after undoing the bow in your hair, unhook your brassiere, and slip the straps over your arms. Now, along with the bra, your dress, with, if you would, all sorts of meanders and flourishes. Perfect."

"Darling, you're mad."

"You're trembling?"

"Yes, a little."

"Perfect."

"Now these?"

Monteaux

"No; before doffing your panties, alphabetical order demands that you take off your garter belt. Perfect. Now your elegant shoes, then your stockings; let them slip slowly over your legs. You will soon see the many fine subtleties I have adjoined to my father's method. Lie down. Using this cord, I will now tie your wrist to that bush. And the other one, if you please. Don't stretch out your arms like that: you look as though you were being crucified. The ankles. Perfect. And now, before proceeding to your execution, several remarks are in order. First of all, let me assure you that any attempt to cry out—futile, in any case, thanks to the rustling branches and roaring cascade—would be, by means of a gag formed of your red handkerchief, immediately proscribed.

"To begin, a glance at the family tree. Until that last moment when, with no hope of escape, you finally fell under my power, I feared that your lack of discernment was simply a ruse. For all your beauty and charm, and despite your small triumph in the laboratory, I am surprised that the vast enemy army chose an agent such as you for so delicate a mission. How could you not have seen that my father and the watchman of the Garden of Oppositions were but one and the same? Is Asilus not a fairly obvious anagram of Lasius? There was no realist counterattack, such as Epsilon might have evoked: in that journal, obviously, the biography has been fictionalized . . . And while it is true that, out of well-justified prudence, my father sought to keep a distance between us by placing me for many years in a boarding school, it was

Monteaux

not without previously filling my mind with a dangerous knowledge, through all manner of secret metaphors whose meaning gradually dawned as I read the account in his suitcase. That an enemy spy, perhaps aided by complicitous police agents and an ambulance, might likely be sent to frustrate the quest for the formidable ink, my father's writings, in their ambiguity, did not fail to warn me."

In a grave voice, labored and breathy, Atta interrupts:

"My mistake, just now, was to have made use of a metaphor. Your madness was in no way a figurative one: with horror, I now see revealed in you, indisputably, the pyromaniac recently escaped from the asylum. And that, beyond all doubt, is why, evoking a thousand contrived pretexts, you proved so little inclined, earlier on, to go to Belcroix."

"You remember such details? Perfect. But patience: on that score, when the time is right, you will hear all the requisite clarifications. Flamboyantly parading, not without insolence, the color red, you called yourself to my attention; soon your knowledge, your lies, an oft-artificial vocabulary, the ardor with which you so frequently fired my senses, all convinced me of your role."

"But why have the minuscule armies not tried before to capture that fearsome insecticide?"

"Because, save certain morbidly sensitive cases, only fitfully controllable, the ants' directives can never transcend the allegorical plane. When at last you were unmasked, I had the idea of

Monteaux

avenging my father, after the fact, by exterminating you with all sorts of meanders and flourishes. And since you displayed such a burning desire, and later, more literally, took me for a pyromaniac, all evidence suggests that you have already imagined the ceremony's details. Had some manner of doubt beset me in the course of my journey, I would have found, in the view photographed at Belcroix, an unimpeachable proof. Such is the angle of the shot— in no way fortuitous, as the director revealed—that the calvary seems, in a sense, to strike out the inscription behind it, formed of blue letters painted onto the ruddy wall enclosing a group of enormous constructions. It is nonetheless possible to read *Labora* ... *re A. C.*, and hence to deduce that it is the syllable *toi* that the monument's shaft has obliterated. Now, a cross can be used both to indicate and to annul. In this case, I believe the latter reading is the one to be favored. Another return to the origin: more than once, it has been necessary to let the Latin tongue intervene in the French. So must we do here, once again, producing the following sentence: to work (*laborare*) in accordance with the directives of Albert Crucis (A.C.) means (the obliteration of the syllable *toi*) making *you* disappear. And I do not doubt that your recent use of the formal *vous* is an attempt to evade that command."

"However painful it may be for both of us, dear Olivier, allow me to reveal my voice's true nature. How to go on denying the obvious truth, how to challenge the irrefutable evidence surrounding

Monteaux

us on all sides? The anagram, for example, unmasking Lasius as Asilus? Nor has the visitor failed to note, a bit further on, apart from the Lasius alienus of the laboratory, that miniature confinement in a boarding school.

"Every stop of the journey can be seen on the square of Belcroix, facing the asylum. It is not difficult to envision, on the fourth floor, a man imprisoned for his pyromania. He is alone. Like a checkerboard, the expanse before him is divided into sixty-four squares by the window's horizontal and vertical bars. The young man muses. He discovers a meaning in the fortuitous superimposition of a cross and a sign. A strange little book enshrined in his memory allows him to expand this phantasmagoria; in the end, having reduced her to impotence, he thinks himself able to vanquish, splendidly undressed and soon consenting, the woman born of his delirium."

"Enough! Truly, this exceeds all bounds: an hallucination exposing itself as such via the mouth of its most charming materialization! No, Atta, it is you who have lost, prematurely, your reason. And I am not so naive as to conceal that Epsilon would have assimilated your attempt to an allegory of the novel's reflexive self-disclosure. Inflamed by this theory, there is no doubt that, in the novelized nature of the paternal biography, in certain passages' occasional word for word reiterations, in the importance, ever greater, granted our personages and their intimacy, in the mounting artificiality distancing our dialogues from all realist

Monteaux

verisimilitude, he would have celebrated the novel's final victory over the guidebook.

"But in fact, it is all far simpler than that. The pyromaniac, Gallois' son, did not escape, it is true, without my aid. Well concealed in the environs, he now awaits my forthcoming signal. In a few moments, I will pull a number of nettle plants from the ground and gather them into a long bouquet, soon ravaging the leaves and stems with great blows against your thighs. This flagellation's first effects will begin to appear, with rapid red welts and swellings spreading over your flesh. With this I will explain why the ants have found vengeance. Next, with all sorts of meanders and flourishes, I will smear you with a fine coating of honey. By their thousands, millions, and billions, creating myriad arborescences around you, toward you, the ants will advance, shrouding your body from head to toe with their brisk pullulations."

"There have been nothing but red ants in these parts for some time now . . ."

"Nevertheless, the honey will whip them into a frenzy. Then, with the aid of meticulously arranged twigs, I will position the magnifying glass such that, at noon, when the solar heat is at its most blazing, the rays will converge onto a patch doused with benzene. All around, the ground will have been laid to guide the spreading flames along eight trajectories. When, tomorrow or the day after, the newspapers report that, from the fire, with its trunks of flame and boughs of smoke, emerged the image—magnified,

Monteaux

mobile, and final—of the obliterated forest, I will be far away. Prudently, I will name the site of the pyromaniac's lair. Ill people are never harshly sentenced: he will merely be guarded and cared for with greater attention. If, in spite of my alibi, some doubt subsists, it will not be too difficult, by anonymous letter, to realize *The Garden of Oppositions*' accusatory aims. Certain passages will be extracted: 'It was her dress that first stopped me, for—red, flowing, elegant—it was made of a fabric quick to evoke, with her every slight movement, a tall, mobile flame,' or, better yet, 'I followed the young female until her moving red silhouette disappeared, among the visitors' green dresses and brown suits, into a more frequented area . . .'

"Sometimes, perhaps, the traveler will have thought of you not as a young female, but rather, in a telling lapsus, as a young flame. If not, let him consider the thesis put forth at the start of the visit, blaming the fire 'on the cross's flamboyant red hues, escaped from their geometric prison.' And so, from quotation to quotation, everywhere finding that I am a mere servile accessory, he will understand, in all the many presages that condemn you, Atta, my despair."

Not far away, crouched over the source of the Damier, Albert Crucis remarks:

"Once again, all this, today, is a metaphor."

And he gazes into the far fictive distance, contemplating the thick layers of white.

126

Selected Dalkey Archive Paperbacks

PETROS ABATZOGLOU, *What Does Mrs. Freeman Want?*
PIERRE ALBERT-BIROT, *Grabinoulor*
YUZ ALESHKOVSKY, *Kangaroo*
FELIPE ALFAU, *Chromos* * *Locos*
IVAN ÂNGELO, *The Celebration* * *The Tower of Glass*
DAVID ANTIN, *Talking*
ALAIN ARIAS-MISSON, *Theatre of Incest*
DJUNA BARNES, *Ladies Almanack* * *Ryder*
JOHN BARTH, *LETTERS* * *Sabbatical*
DONALD BARTHELME, *The King* * *Paradise*
SVETISLAV BASARA, *Chinese Letter*
MARK BINELLI, *Sacco and Vanzetti Must Die!*
ANDREI BITOV, *Pushkin House*
LOUIS PAUL BOON, *Chapel Road* * *Summer in Termuren*
ROGER BOYLAN, *Killoyle*
IGNÁCIO DE LOYOLA BRANDÃO, *Teeth under the Sun* * *Zero*
BONNIE BREMSER, *Troia: Mexican Memoirs*
CHRISTINE BROOKE-ROSE, *Amalgamemnon*
BRIGID BROPHY, *In Transit*
MEREDITH BROSNAN, *Mr. Dynamite*
GERALD L. BRUNS, *Modern Poetry and the Idea of Language*
EVGENY BUNIMOVICH AND J. KATES, EDS., *Contemporary Russian Poetry: An Anthology*
GABRJELLE BURTON, *Heartbreak Hotel*
MICHEL BUTOR, *Degrees* * *Mobile* * *Portrait of the Artist as a Young Ape*
G. CABRERA INFANTE, *Infante's Inferno* * *Three Trapped Tigers*
JULIETA CAMPOS, *The Fear of Losing Eurydice*
ANNE CARSON, *Eros the Bittersweet*
CAMILO JOSÉ CELA, *Christ versus Arizona* * *The Family of Pascual Duarte* * *The Hive*
LOUIS-FERDINAND CÉLINE, *Castle to Castle* * *Conversations with Professor Y* * *London Bridge* * *North* * *Rigadoon*
HUGO CHARTERIS, *The Tide Is Right*
JEROME CHARYN, *The Tar Baby*
MARC CHOLODENKO, *Mordechai Schamz*
EMILY HOLMES COLEMAN, *The Shutter of Snow*
ROBERT COOVER, *A Night at the Movies*
STANLEY CRAWFORD, *Some Instructions to My Wife*
ROBERT CREELEY, *Collected Prose*
RENÉ CREVEL, *Putting My Foot in It*
RALPH CUSACK, *Cadenza*
SUSAN DAITCH, *L.C.* * *Storytown*
NIGEL DENNIS, *Cards of Identity*
PETER DIMOCK, *A Short Rhetoric for Leaving the Family*
ARIEL DORFMAN, *Konfidenz*
COLEMAN DOWELL, *The Houses of Children* * *Island People* * *Too Much Flesh and Jabez*
RIKKI DUCORNET, *The Complete Butcher's Tales* * *The Fountains of Neptune* * *The Jade Cabinet* * *Phosphor in Dreamland* * *The Stain* * *The Word "Desire."*
WILLIAM EASTLAKE, *The Bamboo Bed* * *Castle Keep* * *Lyric of the Circle Heart*
JEAN ECHENOZ, *Chopin's Move*
STANLEY ELKIN, *A Bad Man* * *Boswell: A Modern Comedy* * *Criers and Kibitzers, Kibitzers and Criers* * *The Dick Gibson Show* * *The Franchiser* * *George Mills* * *The Living End* * *The MacGuffin* * *The Magic Kingdom* *

Mrs. Ted Bliss * *The Rabbi of Lud* * *Van Gogh's Room at Arles*
ANNIE ERNAUX, *Cleaned Out*
LAUREN FAIRBANKS, *Muzzle Thyself* * *Sister Carrie*
LESLIE A. FIEDLER, *Love and Death in the American Novel*
GUSTAVE FLAUBERT, *Bouvard and Pécuchet*
FORD MADOX FORD, *The March of Literature*
JON FOSSE, *Melancholy*
MAX FRISCH, *I'm Not Stiller* * *Man in the Holocene*
CARLOS FUENTES, *Christopher Unborn* * *Distant Relations* * *Terra Nostra* * *Where the Air Is Clear*
JANICE GALLOWAY, *Foreign Parts* * *The Trick Is to Keep Breathing*
WILLIAM H. GASS, *A Temple of Texts* * *The Tunnel* * *Willie Masters' Lonesome Wife*
ETIENNE GILSON, *The Arts of the Beautiful* * *Forms and Substances in the Arts*
C. S. GISCOMBE, *Giscome Road* * *Here*
DOUGLAS GLOVER, *Bad News of the Heart* * *The Enamoured Knight*
WITOLD GOMBROWICZ, *A Kind of Testament*
KAREN ELIZABETH GORDON, *The Red Shoes*
GEORGI GOSPODINOV, *Natural Novel*
JUAN GOYTISOLO, *Count Julian* * *Marks of Identity*
PATRICK GRAINVILLE, *The Cave of Heaven*
HENRY GREEN, *Blindness* * *Concluding* * *Doting* * *Nothing*
JIŘÍ GRUŠA, *The Questionnaire*
GABRIEL GUDDING, *Rhode Island Notebook*
JOHN HAWKES, *Whistlejacket*
AIDAN HIGGINS, *A Bestiary* * *Bornholm Night-Ferry* * *Flotsam and Jetsam* * *Langrishe, Go Down* * *Scenes from a Receding Past* * *Windy Arbours*
ALDOUS HUXLEY, *Antic Hay* * *Crome Yellow* * *Point Counter Point* * *Those Barren Leaves* * *Time Must Have a Stop*
MIKHAIL IOSSEL AND JEFF PARKER, EDS., *Amerika: Contemporary Russians View the United States*
GERT JONKE, *Geometric Regional Novel*
JACQUES JOUET, *Mountain R*
HUGH KENNER, *The Counterfeiters* * *Flaubert, Joyce and Beckett: The Stoic Comedians* * *Joyce's Voices*
DANILO KIŠ, *Garden, Ashes* * *A Tomb for Boris Davidovich*
AIKO KITAHARA, *The Budding Tree: Six Stories of Love in Edo*
ANITA KONKKA, *A Fool's Paradise*
GEORGE KONRÁD, *The City Builder*
TADEUSZ KONWICKI, *A Minor Apocalypse* * *The Polish Complex*
MENIS KOUMANDAREAS, *Koula*
ELAINE KRAF, *The Princess of 72nd Street*
JIM KRUSOE, *Iceland*
EWA KURYLUK, *Century 21*
VIOLETTE LEDUC, *La Bâtarde*
DEBORAH LEVY, *Billy and Girl* * *Pillow Talk in Europe and Other Places*
JOSÉ LEZAMA LIMA, *Paradiso*
ROSA LIKSOM, *Dark Paradise*
OSMAN LINS, *Avalovara* * *The Queen of the Prisons of Greece*

Selected Dalkey Archive Paperbacks

For a full list of publications, visit WWW.DALKEYARCHIVE.COM